THE DEMON KING'S
LIBRARIAN
EverEri

CONTENT WARNING

The content in this book may not be suitable for everyone. Please be aware that this book contains the following: Explicit sex scenes

To Mana, the inspiration for Tareen. Your passion for these books has been an inspiration, and I hope you love the little witch.

To all you neurospicy beans out there. In a world that makes you feels different, never forget that you deserved to be loved just as much as anyone else.

Chapter 1

I weaved in and out of bookshelves, counting 20 in total—less than usual. The library was feeling shy today. Or it wanted to play games. Both moods often led to the same results. The entire section on elven history was nowhere in sight, not like it had been yesterday. That was the downside to having a living library. I hadn't intended to give it life when I created it, but that often happened with my magic. It was powerful but had uncontrollable side effects.

I pressed my hand into my side and breathed as deeply as I could manage—which wasn't much at all. My lungs hated me. My entire body hated me. I pinched the fat on my side, wishing I was skinny and didn't have all of these health problems. I had spent centuries imagining how much better life would have been if I had been different.

"Where are my books?" I demanded. If anyone heard me speaking to the library, they might have thought I was crazy. Living libraries were unheard of, even in a world ruled by demons and magic. It was incredible how narrow-minded beings were when there were demons who could walk through shadows and light ruling the world.

The bookshelves shifted in taunt. The library was feeling cheeky today, but I didn't have the energy to deal with it.

I huffed, dramatically rolling my eyes. I didn't know if the room had the ability to see my annoyed gesture, but I liked to think it did. If it was going to be stubborn, then I was going to be dramatic.

"I give up."

I stalked back to my room, resigned to continue my research on the elves another day. History wouldn't change if I waited a few days.

I knocked on a blank wall twice. An enchanted door opened, revealing the hallway to my room. I didn't like people in my space, so I kept the entrance hidden. In an estate filled with rejects and misfits, it was often difficult to find complete privacy, especially when the library was free to use. It was the property of the demon king, since it was his estate, and he was allowing me to live at Ethlow for free.

My room was a different story. Even if the walls belonged to the demon king, it was my space. I didn't want people to touch my stuff without my permission, especially if I wasn't there to monitor them. Most importantly, I didn't like it when others saw the messy state of my room. I hated cleaning, and my private quarters reflected that.

A soft meow pulled my attention as Binx came out of hiding, flicking his black tail as he approached. He jumped onto the back of the couch and rubbed his head against my side, forcing me to stop to pet him. He only came out of hiding when I was alone. He didn't like others, which I understood. I didn't like most beings. It was easier being alone.

"The library is in a mood today, which means no research." I didn't know if Binx understood my words any more than the library did, but he nuzzled against my palm, urging me to keep petting him.

Binx had been my companion since before I arrived at the demon king's estate over a century ago. My magic had extended my human life, something I hadn't had control over. But when Binx found me over a century ago, I cast a spell on him to make him live as long as me. I couldn't stand the thought of losing him before my time. With him by my side, I never felt alone.

"I guess I can read one of my books in here and hang out with you."

Binx meowed in approval, so it was settled. I grabbed a book off the pile next to my bed titled *When the Mountains Turned Cold* and dove into my romance about a human man falling in love with an ancient witch. It was one of my favorites. I loved reading about love, knowing it was never in the cards for me.

No one stuck around long with a witch who had a tendency to be a little too blunt. Maybe if I was pretty and athletic, they could look past my personality, but my body was round, and I couldn't count my health issues on a single hand. What a joke? An immortal witch who struggled to breathe without her bimonthly treatments.

I had thought magic would fix my ailments, but it had made them worse. At least the demon king's estate had been a reprieve from the human villages who hunted me down. It was incredible how long humans had managed to survive in a world filled with magic. They were like cockroaches, thriving in the worst conditions. Cockroaches who believed any magic was the work of evil demons—even when the potions I had made had nothing to do with real magic.

Humans had learned to accept magic and demons since they tried to burn me at the stake, but I never forgot what they did to me. I glanced at my thighs where the scars lingered beneath the black fabric. A permanent reminder of the fire that licked my legs before I managed to escape the claws of the village I had called home in another life.

Yet another thing my magic couldn't fix.

I settled on the couch, ready to lose myself in my book. Binx jumped on my stomach and curled up, loving the soft roundness of it. It was the perfect place for a cat to nap. As much as I hated my body, I loved Binx too much to fault him for using me as a pillow. He could commit the gravest of sins, and I wouldn't find fault in him.

I cracked my book open to reveal the scrap of paper I used to mark my place, but before my eyes could process the words, the air went tight. Wards I had placed some time ago pulled in warning. Someone was in the library. Someone with incredible power.

All magic had a different feel and taste, and I had tasted this magic before. Once. I had never met the demon in person, but he had left his scent all over my library. I slammed my book shut, anger building. Months I had waited for this opportunity. I had expected him to return within a week after the incident, but as time went by without the demon's presence, the incident slid to the back of my head.

I left my book on the couch as I stormed out of my room, ignoring the tickle in my throat from the sudden movement. The magic burned my nose as I stepped into the library. The door to my room sealed automatically. The last thing I needed was for *him* to know where I slept.

I followed the scent of berries on a winter breeze to the main room where it was the strongest. A demon stood tall as his eyes scanned a bookshelf. Large horns curled out of his head covered in spikes. Pointed ears poked through his thick black hair. A black button-up shirt stretched over his chest, barely containing his ripped muscles. It didn't contain the large feathered wings that originated from between his shoulder blades.

"What are you doing here?" I demanded, stopping in the center of the room.

"Is that any way to speak to a demon king?" He turned slowly, revealing a mouth full of sharp teeth and glowing purple eyes. He was the type of demon that haunted the nightmares of humans. His power was thick and unyielding, the kind that could rip a life away without remorse.

"Jathral," I said, knowing exactly who stood in my room.

"That's King Jathral to you." His eyes sparkled, treachery lying beneath the vivid color.

"I don't care if you're a king or a peasant. You're not welcome here." Demons didn't scare me. I had lived long enough to face horrors worse than an arrogant demon who thought he could push others around because of a simple title.

His smile dropped as he took a step closer. "If you don't want to face my wrath, witch—"

"I'll do nothing," I interrupted. "I do not answer to you. I live under the protection of King Zathrian. Even if I didn't, I would never submit to someone like you. You destroyed my library, so get out." I pointed to the door, my own power surging. Books flipped open, and wind ruffled my hair.

"You are nothing compared to me, a mere mouse among snakes. If you know what's best for you, you will not challenge me." He stepped forward until he was inches away.

I had to strain my neck to look up at him with his towering height. He was the kind of asshole who thought he could bully me into submission because I was a short human woman. Pathetic. Weak. Ugly. That was what I had been called all my mortal life. I couldn't change my feeble body or the shape of my face, but I was no longer pathetic. The power pulsing through my veins proved that.

I jammed my finger into the demon king's muscular chest. "I'm not afraid of you, so get the fuck out of my library before I show you exactly what I can do." I released a wave of electricity, lighting the room up with magic. My curly hair poofed with the energy pulsing from me, but I didn't care about my looks.

Jathral curled his lip back, revealing four sharp canines that could easily puncture my skin. "I will be back, and I will get what I want. I always do."

"Not this time," I said, crossing my arms and standing as tall as my short body allowed.

He snarled as his body erupted into flames. He disappeared in the flash of heat, but not before setting a book on fire. I waved my hand, suffocating the flames with magic. My hands shook as anger twisted in my blood. If I thought I hated Jathral before, I despised him now.

Chapter 2

S atella's brows furrowed when she saw me. "What did you do to yourself now?" The healer had been at the estate for over fifty years, and in that time, she had treated my various ailments. She was the best non-magical healer I had ever worked with.

I pressed my hand against my chest. "My breathing is bad today."

Her face softened at the admission. She scolded me when I came in for accidents, saying I was too reckless when my potions exploded or when I crashed my broom. She never judged when it came to my weak lungs. I wondered if that would have changed if I told her the truth about why they were so weak. Using magic drained my body, and since my lungs had been weak when I gained my powers, that was the first part of my body that strained under the weight of my magic. The more I used my powers, the worse my lung function grew.

If I wasn't careful, one day it would kill me. I wasn't sure if that was such a bad thing. I had already lived long past what my mortal lifespan was supposed to be. Longer than any other witch I knew.

Satella gestured for me to sit while she prepared the breathing treatment. I focused on moving my lungs, but it did little to stop the wheezing. The vampire glanced at me out of the corner of her eyes, worry lacing her face. I didn't want her pity, but part of me was grateful for her concern. If I were to fall into the grasps of the underworld, she would notice I was missing. The rest of the world wouldn't, but knowing there was at least one person out there who cared warmed my soul.

Satella urged me to sit over the boiling cauldron. I inhaled the steam infused with herbs, and with each breath, my body eased a little more.

"Slow, deep breaths," the vampire said, but it was unnecessary. We had been doing this every other week for nearly five decades. I knew how the process worked, but I bit back my comment. Satella was only doing her job.

"How's your girlfriend?" I asked between breaths. My throat protested, sending me into a small coughing fit.

Satella rubbed my back and gave me a look that said, *Don't speak.*

"Astoria is good." The vampire bit her lip and turned her face away in an attempt to hide her giddiness. "She's been busy, but I'm supposed to see her tonight."

Satella hadn't been in a serious relationship during her time at the estate until recently. She had had plenty of flings. Someone with a body like hers could get anyone she wanted, but it wasn't until a grim reaper showed up and stole her heart that the vampire finally settled into a relationship.

I wished it was that easy for me. I wasn't single by choice. Not fully. I had tried to find a relationship for a long time, but most guys barely noticed me. Despite having a larger body, it was as if the extra layers of fat turned me invisible to the male species. And the ones who did see me didn't have a nice thing to say. Eventually, I stopped trying. It was easier to be independent and lonely than to be ridiculed for wanting someone to care about me.

"You two are cute together." The grim reaper didn't come around often, but when she was free, she occasionally joined us for dinner.

Most days, I ate dinner with Satella and her group of friends. It was a little strange eating with others, since I had spent most of my time at Ethlow eating alone, but Satella had invited me to eat with her and the others a few weeks ago. Out of politeness, I hadn't wanted to say no. Weeks had passed with me joining them, but I didn't feel like I fully belonged in that group of friends. Sometimes I wondered if I received the invite out of pity, but the others always welcomed me with bright smiles. If they were acting, they were good at it.

"Don't say stuff like that." Satella scrunched her nose. She brushed off most compliments she received.

Silence filled the air as I focused on my breathing, the ache in my lungs lessening with each breath. I shouldn't have used magic to show off to Jathral. He didn't deserve the sacrifice it took to use that kind of power, but I hated that he thought he could push me around. I wanted to put the asshole in his place.

"Aukina has been talking about wanting to go to the lake as a group before it gets much colder." Satella turned to work on what she had been doing before I arrived. She crushed herbs in a stone bowl using a steady motion. "It's probably too cold to swim in the lake, especially with winter right around the corner, but it'd be nice to get out of the estate as a group."

I blinked a few times, unsure if she was talking about plans with her friends or if she was inviting me. I decided to take the safe route. "I'm sure you guys will have fun."

Satella paused to look at me. "Aren't you going to join?"

I rocked back and forth, acting as if I needed a moment to catch my breath before responding. "I haven't left the estate in a while." I didn't want her to feel obligated to invite me, so I tried to give her an out.

"Then it's settled. You'll come with us. I'll let you know when we figure out the specific day." The healer beamed brightly. If she caught on to my insecurity about the invite, she didn't show it.

I took a deep breath in an attempt to settle my nerves. It did little to help, but at least I didn't break out into a coughing fit. I wasn't good with people, but Satella seemed intent on getting me involved with her little group of friends.

The demon king's office was simpler than I remembered. I pulled at my fingers as I waited for Zathrian to appear. It had been a long time since the demon king summoned me to his office. We had a general agreement. He left me to run the library in peace. I didn't ask him for anything in return. It was a good agreement, neither of us worrying about the other. The demon king had too much on his plate, and I didn't like anyone telling me what to do.

There were only two reasons I could think of for why I was called to his office.

"Good morning, Miss Tareen." Shadows flickered, and then the master of the house, Viridian, stood next to the demon king's desk. He was the one who had left the summons on my door first thing in the morning.

"Good morning, Viridian," I said. He didn't like it when the residents of Ethlow dropped his title of "Master," but he allowed me to get away with it. It was the advantage of knowing who the demon truly was. All of my research on the Great Demon Wars had left me clues about his identity, and when I had called him out on it, he didn't deny it.

"I trust you know why you were summoned today," the demon asked. His teal eyes glowed, and his bat-winged horns twitched.

I tilted my head. "I'm fairly certain that whatever Zathrian wishes to speak to me about is a waste of my time."

Viridian's lips showed a phantom smile. I had never seen the demon properly smile, but occasionally his lip twitched up. "I tried to tell the young sire that, but he has his role to play."

I intertwined my fingers and leaned back, trying to appear more relaxed than I felt. "We all have our roles to play, don't we?"

"Indeed." The demon's eyes flashed, no other communication necessary.

The door opened a moment later, and Zathrian walked in, wearing a dark shirt with a gold tie that matched the inlets in his horns. He was just as tall as Jathral—maybe there was something about being a demon king that made their bodies especially large—but

Zathrian's shoulders were wider. He tucked in his leathery wings as he moved to the throne-like chair behind his desk.

His power filled the air in erratic but strong waves, but his smile was nothing like how the rumors spun the demon king. He was barely a demon with the way he acted, always smiling and seeing the positive in the world. His teeth were bright white as he smiled. He was older than me, but sometimes it was difficult to see that when he acted too nicely.

"Good morning, Tareen. How are you today?" The demon king was lucky Viridian agreed to be his second in command, otherwise he would've let himself get walked all over by the selfish rulers of the world.

"Same as usual. Why am I here?" I tried not to flinch at my own terse voice. I didn't mean to sound harsh and blunt, but I was ready to get back to the library in hopes the shelves would allow me to continue my research on the history of the elves during the Great Demon War.

Zathrian cleared his throat and shifted in his chair. "King Jathral is here for a visit, and he requested use of the library. I granted him access. I didn't think about informing you, so I understand why his presence might have thrown you off."

I huffed. Jathral was even more pathetic than I thought. When I said no, he went above my head. "No. He is not allowed in my library." Bold. Such a bold statement to the king of Kinzlea. I understood that, but it didn't stop my sharp tone.

Viridian stepped forward, his shadow magic flickering off his shoulders. It was all for show. He wouldn't use it against me unless

I posed a threat to the king or his estate. "Might I remind you that it is not your library? You are merely minding it."

Zathrian held up his hand, silencing the powerful demon at his side. Viridian's eyes flickered with ire, but he did not argue.

"Why?" the king asked.

I blinked, shocked he didn't come to the proper conclusion on his own. "Have you forgotten the incident where Jathral nearly killed the woman you love and destroyed parts of the library in the process?"

The king tensed. His golden eyes retreated to a darkness that had rarely touched him since he fell in love with Nyri, a simple human descended from a line of powerful witches.

When he didn't answer, I pressed forward. "While I understand and respect your authority, you gave me the library to protect it. I have done that and built it into something worthy of calling a library instead of a stack of books. I will not allow Jathral to use what is precious to me until he makes up for what he did."

Whatever darkness lingered in the demon king's eyes disappeared. He cleared his throat, bringing himself back to the present. "So if he makes up for what he did, he can use the library?"

I wanted to say no, but I was mildly aware of the power Zathrian had over me. He could kick me out of Ethlow for insubordination if I flat out refused him. I doubted Zathrian would resort to such a threat, but the shadow demon next to him wouldn't hesitate to hold it over my head. I had known Viridian long enough to know what the demon was capable of.

"I suppose," I answered after a long moment.

"How?"

I didn't understand why Zathrian was so eager to help someone like Jathral out. I didn't need to know the demon king of Mithcourt to know exactly who he was. An entitled prick who liked to wave his dick around to prove to everyone just how powerful he was.

"Tell him to figure it out on his own." I stood up, smoothing my long black skirt. "I'm done here."

I walked away without looking back. The demons in charge of the estate could kick me out, but I would not give Jathral what he wanted until he earned it.

Chapter 3

I dusted the top of the bookshelves while sitting on my broom to reach higher. As the dust in the air gathered, a sneeze built up in my nose. I tried to push it back, but my body was too weak to fight the instinct. The sneeze made my entire body shudder, and my broom spun out of control. I barely managed to dodge the bookshelf behind me, which would have resulted in at least one of the shelves falling.

"That's why I don't like cleaning," I said to no one in particular. I tried to keep the library clean, but the sheer size made it nearly impossible on my own. The library stretched four stories high with balconies and ladders at each level to allow access. I rarely needed to access the higher levels. It was as if the library knew what books visitors would need on the rare visits. It liked to rearrange the shelves, so the desired content was available on the first floor.

Unless the library was acting ornery. Then it hid the elven history from the librarian for no good reason.

The air went taut, as if some god was pulling a bow string, ready to send an arrow my way. I held back the internal groan. I knew Jathral would show up sooner or later after my conversation with the demon king. A few days passed in silence, and I had hoped

Jathral's pride was bigger than his need to use my library. I wasn't lucky enough for that to happen.

I should've known better. The library at Ethlow was the best collection in all of Kinzlea. It was better than any library in all five of the demon-ruled kingdoms. I had made sure of that in the century I had spent at the demon king's estate. Knowledge was power, and if I was going to spend the rest of my useless life at Ethlow, then I wanted the knowledge of the world at my fingertips.

When the information wasn't being hidden by the library itself.

I counted the seconds as I waited for Jathral to call out to me. When I wasn't at the desk in the front of the library, visitors reached out for assistance. It was unnecessary, since the wards I had on the room warned me the moment someone entered, but most weren't aware of the magic that flowed in the room.

Several moments passed without a word from the demon king. My chest tightened, frustration building. If the king of Mithcourt thought he could get away with using the library without my permission, I would have to teach him a lesson.

I flew on my broom, racing towards the front, ready to smack Jathral around. I expected him to be searching the shelves for whatever coveted information he wanted. Instead, he sat at my desk with his feet propped up. His hands clasped behind his head, and his eyes flicked to mine, making brief eye contact.

It was enough to distract me, and I found myself crashing into a pile of books. I tumbled into hard surfaces and knew my body would be covered in bruises later—not an unusual occurrence for me.

The low chuckle that emerged from Jathral's throat had me seeing red. He didn't bother to offer help as I struggled to my feet. My chest heaved up and down, and I clenched my fingers, glaring at the demon king.

"Get out of my chair, and then get out of my library." My chest turned to ice as my magic swirled inside me at dangerous levels. It wanted to exact revenge on the demon king more than I did, but I was careful to keep it leashed. After flying, my body was dangerously low on strength. If I didn't eat something before expending more magic, I would end up nauseous and spilling my guts everywhere. Or unable to breathe. It was a gamble for which ailment would strike my body after using a surge of magic unprepared.

Jathral tilted his head. "You really don't comprehend that you are nothing but a mouse, and I am ready to strike at a moment's notice. You won't even see the strike coming."

Perhaps I should've quivered at the demon's threat, but I wasn't afraid of him. If he wanted to, he could kill me, but I wasn't afraid of death. He studied my eyes, and his brows lifted as if he could sense my indifference.

"You don't seem to understand that this is my library, and you can't intimidate me into giving you what you want." I placed my hands on my hips, determined not to waver.

I was taller than Jathral when he sat, but just barely. Despite the height advantage, he didn't look the slightest bit concerned about what I was saying.

"Yes, Zathrian told me you expected me to grovel." He picked up a book and cracked it open, scanning the text inside.

I waved my hand, using an invisible force to snatch the book from his hands. "Groveling wouldn't hurt, but I doubt there's anything you can do to convince me to let you use my library. You'll have better luck going elsewhere."

He pulled his feet off the desk, making his movements dramatic. He towered over me and stepped closer. I backed up automatically, not wanting him to invade my personal space. My back hit the wall, but that didn't stop Jathral from encroaching closer.

"This is how this is going to work, little mouse." He used his pointer finger to lift my chin, forcing me to look into his eyes. "I am going to use the library as I please, and you won't get in my way. I get what I want, and you don't get hurt. Understood?"

"There's one problem with your plan." I kept my face flat, even as my magic swirled in my chest, begging me to release it.

His lips pulled into a crooked smile. "And what's that?"

I brought my knee between his legs and shoved my hands against his chest, releasing the burst of magic that had been begging to put the demon king in his place. Jathral flew backwards, landing on his ass. "I bite back."

I stalked past him, not bothering to acknowledge the shocked expression on his face. I waved my hand, and a shield appeared behind me, blocking the demon king from every book in the library, except the one on my desk. Jathral made a grave mistake going against me. He took one look and saw a clumsy, feeble witch. He assumed he was better than me just because he was a demon king, and I was a witch who found herself hiding from the world in the demon king's estate.

But if the king of Mithcourt didn't realize it now, he would quickly learn that I was no simple witch with weak magic.

"Touch a book again, and my magic will render you unconscious. Try it if you don't believe me. I'd love to see you in pain." I kept walking, hoping Jathral was too shocked to notice the wobble in my legs.

I didn't stop moving until I was safely behind the hidden door to my room. Only then did I drop to my knees, my body too exhausted to make it to my couch. I reached up and touched my nose, wiping the blood leaking from it. It was deep red and flowed steadily. My magic was powerful, but it always came at a cost. Showing Jathral I was not just some mouse he could push around was worth the toll it took on my body.

Binx meowed, appearing from the shadows. He nudged my arm, checking on me. He always knew when I pushed my body too far. I should've gone directly to Satella. She would've been able to help me, but that would also require admitting to her the truth about my ailments. As far as she knew, I was born sickly, and my disease of the lungs was a fact of my life.

It wasn't completely off base. I was born sickly, but the persistence of my sickness was a result of my magic. All magic came at a cost. That was what the demon, Aburon, said to me before I made a pact with him, sealed by my blood. I hadn't cared. At the time, I was desperate for magic to prove I was more than the overweight girl that was unlovable. I had thought any price was worth the magic the demon would bestow on me.

I pressed my sleeve against my nose, grateful for my black shirt since the blood stain wouldn't be noticeable. Slow breaths and time would stop the bleeding. The magic took from me, but it never took more than what my body could handle. A part of me hoped it would sustain me for an eternity, but deep down, I knew the clock was ticking. It'd be a matter of time before the magic took more than I could handle, and I'd end up in the underworld.

Chapter 4

I didn't go to dinner with the others for a few days. It took that long for my body to recover after putting up the wards to stop Jathral from entering the library. If he had been anyone else, even a lesser demon, it wouldn't have taken as much out of me as it did. But putting up wards to stop a demon king from touching an entire library took every ounce of power I had, and it felt as if I had had an allergic reaction to the demon king. It had been awhile since I had used that much power, but last time, I had recovered faster.

I didn't have the energy to socialize after that, which I didn't mind. I liked the quietness of the library and the vast knowledge at my fingertips.

"Hello?" a familiar voice called out.

My body tensed. I was grateful for the soft female voice and the lack of demon essence, but I didn't know why Aukina was at the library. She rarely visited. As a mermaid, she grew up in the Hallow Sea, and they didn't read like we did on land. She had learned how to read common since coming to the demon king's estate, but I had never seen her reading for pleasure.

"Coming!" I called out. I didn't use my broom today, not wanting to expend any unnecessary magic until I was back to normal health. It took longer to make it to the front, but Aukina waited patiently.

The mermaid looked around, her gills flaring as she stared at the stacks and stacks of books. It wasn't her first time in the library, but she looked at the place with wonderment every time. I noted her appreciation, tucking it away in my trove of opinions. I liked the mermaid, even if I didn't know her well.

When Aukina sensed my approach, she shifted her attention to me, but her dark eyes didn't lose their sparkle. She tossed her thick black hair over her shoulder before holding out a dish.

"I thought I'd bring you some food, since you haven't joined us recently." She looked at me expectantly, waiting for me to take her offering.

I hesitated, thrown off by her kind gesture. The mermaid had been at Ethlow for nearly six years, but we had barely spoken until recently. Until Satella invited me to join their little group for dinner. It was strange being part of something like that. In most ways, I felt like a guest, sitting on the outside of some inner circle. I didn't know what changed my title from guest to friend.

I took the dish, glancing down at the different muffins. Friends did things like bring each other food. "Thank you."

I expected Aukina to say, "You're welcome," and walk away, but she lingered, her eyes scanning me closely.

"We've all been worried about you." She shifted on her feet, as if she wasn't comfortable. "If we did something to upset you—"

"No, that's not it," I quickly said. I didn't want her to get the wrong impression. "I haven't been feeling well. That's all."

Aukina pinched her lips together. "Satella said you haven't been to see her either."

They were worried about me. Something about that thought made my chest swell. It had been a long time since someone had cared whether I showed up somewhere. I was used to being on my own and handling my issues in private. But Aukina was concerned. So were the others, if what she said was true.

"When you're chronically ill, you get used to certain things. I don't want to run to Satella every time I'm feeling off." It was a true statement, but it wasn't the real reason I didn't visit the healer. I didn't want her to ask questions about my health, because I wouldn't lie. I didn't want her or anyone else to know the price I paid for my powers. As far as they knew, I was a simple witch born with magic. Nothing more. Nothing less.

Aukina nodded, as if she understood, but I doubted she did. The mermaid had a strong immune system, perhaps inherited as part of her sea-dwelling form.

"Make sure to rest plenty. We want to go to the lake in three days, and we'd love for you to join us."

"Why?" The question came out more bluntly than I intended. I struggled to control my tone, only aware of the harshness after it escaped my mouth. Centuries of keeping to myself hadn't helped.

Aukina smiled, unfazed by my tone. "Because you're our friend, and we want you there." There was nothing mocking in her statement, but I blinked twice, waiting for her to laugh and say it was a joke.

When that didn't happen, I asked, "Is everyone's partner going?" I was happy that the others had found relationships at the estate that took in the unwanted and broken. Nyri with the demon king. Aukina with Reamann, a demon guardsman. Satella with Astoria, a grim reaper of all beings. But it would have been a lie to say I wasn't jealous. Being around all of them with their respective partners wasn't easy. Thankfully, it didn't happen often, since King Zathrian was busy with running a kingdom, and Astoria was busy collecting souls.

"Only Reamann is coming," Aukina said. "The others can't slip away from their responsibilities. Reamann technically should be at his post, but Zathrian didn't want us to go without any kind of protection. That's the advantage of dating one of the most trusted guardsmen."

I nodded, a little surprised the demon king wasn't sending an entire army with us to protect his mate. She had already been threatened twice, once by poisoning, and once by Jathral.

A flash of heat crawled up my neck. I couldn't understand why Zathrian would let someone like *Jathral* enter the demon king's estate willingly.

"That sounds fun," I said before Aukina caught on to my moment of anger.

"Good. Rest up, and I can bring you soup to help. Visit Satella if you need to, because we want you healthy."

I nodded, not having to fake the smile. For centuries, I had been content being alone, but the prospect of friends, real friends, stirred something within me. Something that scared me. Opening up to anyone gave them the opportunity to hurt me.

The lights around the room flickered. They were powered by the demon king's magic, always burning. Even in the night, they merely dimmed when the estate fell into a slumber. There was only one thing that could make the lights flicker.

Aukina's eyes widened, recognizing the power that loomed nearby. Anyone who had spent more than a day at Ethlow could sense when the master of the house was nearby.

"I should get back to work," Aukina said, her eyes darting around. She was the head chef, but it was after dinner, which meant she didn't have any work to do. I didn't correct her, only waving goodbye as she scurried away.

Viridian had that effect on people.

I shook my head, pretending to organize books. Once Aukina was out of earshot, I said, "You get a kick out of scaring the residents, don't you?"

Viridian stepped out of the shadows. His outfit was perfectly pressed, as always. Dark green ruffles framed his neck, the only color in his black formal outfit. In the time I had spent at Ethlow, I had only seen a hair out of place once, but the demon would deny it if I called him out for it.

"I would never take pleasure in scaring the residents of Ethlow." The demon's eyes flickered, the only indication that his words did not hold truth. "I wanted a moment alone with you."

I raised an eyebrow. It wasn't often the demon had business with me. It didn't take a genius to know what the visit was about.

"I'm not allowing him in my library." I turned my back on Viridian and gathered books strewn about on one of the tables. I placed them on a cart, knowing the library would sort the books back to where they belonged when no one was looking.

"I have to say, I'm impressed you didn't fold. Jathral has a way of getting others to do as he pleases." Despite Viridian's words sounding like a compliment, it felt like an insult.

I whirled on the demon, and my body quickly reminded me I hadn't completely recovered from the surge of magic I used to place a ward around the library. "I'm not as weak as you think." All my life, others had underestimated me. Even with the power surging through my veins, they couldn't take me seriously.

"I know you're not weak." Viridian sent a tendril of power towards me. His shadows caressed my skin, making me cringe. I didn't like being touched without permission, even by phantom shadows. "I know exactly how much power you hold in your veins."

The demon seal stamped on my abdomen flared in response to Viridian's magic. The master of the house had a way of knowing things he shouldn't have. It was as if his shadows whispered in his ears, spilling the secrets of the estate.

Viridian turned, his eyes scanning the invisible force field designed to keep only one demon out. "Jathral has been throwing a hissy fit since you threw him out."

"So?" I didn't care how harsh my voice was when it came to Jathral.

A phantom smile crossed Viridian's lips, but a single blink erased the evidence. "It's about time someone knocked him down a peg."

I had prepared myself for a scolding. Not this. Not after how Viridian had spoken to me in Zathrian's office. "Then why are you here?"

"Because whatever the sire wishes for, it is my responsibility to make it happen." Viridian stood as still as a statue. The control he had over his body was impeccable.

"Why lower yourself to such a role? Why fulfill the whimsies of a demon king when you could do so much more?" It wasn't my place to ask such a question, but it didn't stop me. I had been wondering why Viridian promised himself to Zathrian's reign when he could've had freedom.

Viridian was silent for a long while. It made me wonder if he was going to respond at all. It wasn't unusual for the demon to brush off questions he didn't want to answer.

"Because serving someone with a heart like his is not lowering myself. It's an honor to help Zathrian achieve his dreams. If he is successful, then there will be a little less pain in this cruel world." His eyes were distant, but the fact he spoke about the topic was a shock.

I had known of Viridian before he took an oath to Zathrian. The Shadow Slinger had once been rumored to be the most powerful demon in all the mortal realm, possibly more powerful than the ruler of the underworld. Centuries ago, the Shadow Slinger disappeared, time forgetting the demon. I had wondered what happened to him, but after arriving at Ethlow, it hadn't taken me long to put the pieces together.

"And what about you, Miss Tareen? Why are you here instead of using your talents elsewhere?" Viridian tried to throw the difficult question back at me, but I had an easy answer.

"I don't have any talents."

Viridian hummed, but he didn't confirm or deny if he agreed with me. "Do me a favor."

For a moment, I was sure I had hallucinated the demon's words. He didn't ask for favors. He gave out tasks and orders. "A favor?"

"Make Jathral grovel before you give him what he wants." The twinkle in Viridian's eyes said more than enough.

I thought about telling him I wasn't going to give the demon king of Mithcourt what he wanted, but the thought of Jathral groveling sparked something inside of me. "I will."

Chapter 5

I t took Jathral a week before he dared to show his face at the library. Knowing the demon king had spent a week away after our last interaction made my chest warm. I imagined him pacing in a dark room, too scared to face me.

"I didn't know if I was going to see your hideous face again." I didn't bother to look up from my book. It was about the Great Demon War from the perspective of humans, but it was boring and uninformative. Humans were too riddled with pride and fear to be objective when describing history. The book described dangerous beasts that never existed. Likely demons that had been twisted by the fears of mortals.

Jathral ran his hand over his sharp jawline. He was normally clean-shaven, but stubble covered his chin, darkening his features. "I am one of the most handsome demons you have ever seen." There was no hesitation or doubt in his voice. He knew his sculpted features were what women and men fell over themselves for.

Even with his black feathered wings stretched behind him and the horns curling out of his head, he was stunning. Some demons tricked their prey into deals using fear, some prayed on desire. Some charmed them into signing away their souls.

Jathral was the type to use his charms and good looks to pull weak-willed beings into his nefarious deals.

"I've seen better." I wasn't sure if that was true. I was a fool if I denied the demon king's true allure. But I'd never admit it to his face. I was sure he was used to being praised for his looks, and the last thing I wanted to do was build him up.

Jathral huffed a breath through his nose. It was subtle, but it was telling. I was getting under his skin.

"Look, little mouse. I know you think you're clever, but I always get my way. It would be best for you to give up this fight now." He stalked towards me, but I kept my focus on my book, paying him no heed. I felt every step he took, though. His power weaved through the air, making promises of fortune and pleasure.

I cocked an eyebrow at the personality of his magic. It was just as arrogant as the demon attached to it. Did the magic shape the male, or did the male shape the magic? An interesting question to tuck away for later. I would need a young magic user to study that question. Someone like Nyri. She had only discovered her magic half a year ago. She'd make the perfect subject.

Later. That matter wasn't as pressing as tearing down the demon king from his throne of superiority.

"No, thanks." I flipped the page, pretending to scan the words in front of me. The content of the book didn't process, not as Jathral stood over my desk, looking down at me with the hate of a thousand suns.

He placed his hands on the desk and leaned forward. The smell of fresh snow and winter berries washed over me. It was rare to get winter berries in Kinzlea, since they needed the most frigid environments to thrive. They were a delicacy I had the opportunity to indulge in only a few times.

"What do you want, little mouse?"

I lowered the book, finally looking into the demon's dark eyes. Desperation danced in his pupils, but it wasn't enough. I set the book down slowly and leaned forward. Our breaths tangled, leaving little space between our faces.

"You haven't bothered to apologize, but you are asking me what I want?"

His breath was heavy as he fought against himself. He wasn't used to others talking back to him, especially not lowly witches like me. "I don't apologize." The words were hoarse as they escaped. For a moment, he had considered it. Whatever he needed with my library was important enough to falter in his ways, but that wasn't my problem.

"Then you don't get access to my library, and don't think about killing me to break the wards. Even after my death, the protection spell will last, and then you won't have a way to get what you want." I stood, ready to walk away.

Jathral moved to block me. He was a wall of muscle, one that would be impossible for me to move physically. Even if I faced him with the full might of my magic, I wasn't sure I could defeat a demon king if he was prepared for the onslaught. I was better with wards and protection spells than I was with fighting.

But there was one aspect Jathral couldn't beat me in. He might have been stronger physically, but he couldn't break my mind. I had centuries of practice dealing with condescending assholes like him.

I held my chin high, showing him I wasn't afraid. There was nothing he could do to break me.

"This isn't a game, witch. I did not come to my rival's territory and make a deal to use his library for you to stand in the way." The air chilled as he spoke, but my magic reacted, lighting a fire in my soul and keeping me warm.

"You may have made a deal with Zathrian, but this is my library and these are my books. If you want to use them, you'll have to play by my rules." The challenge sparked something deep within me. It had been a long time since I went toe-to-toe with someone like Jathral. For nearly a century, my biggest challenger was Viridian, but the master of the house wasn't as scary as he let the others believe.

"Lives are at stake." Jathral was trying to play the sympathy card, but he was playing it on the wrong being. I had grown hard over the plight of others after the world had pushed me aside for centuries.

"In that case, I expect you to get on your knees and grovel." I held my ground, my heart thundering from the thrill of facing a demon king and knowing the worst he could do to me would have been a welcomed relief.

"Are you that heartless?" Jathral asked. He leaned in closer, grabbing my chin.

I refused to show him an ounce of fear. "Are you that prideful?" I grabbed his hand and pulled it off my face. "Don't touch me without permission."

Jathral clicked his tongue. He didn't try to touch me again, but he didn't give me any breathing room. "I will win you over. I never fail."

"You can try." I slid past Jathral, squeezing between his body and the wall. I stumbled forward, my legs weak from the interaction, but I steadied myself with a hand on my desk. I didn't want the demon king to see how weak my body was.

A low growl resounded in my ear, and then a flash of heat hit my back. Jathral's power disappeared, but the scent of snow and winter berries lingered. I pressed my hand to my chest, my heart thrumming. I knew that wasn't going to be the last time I saw the king of Mithcourt, and a shock of excitement made my blood rush.

He wouldn't break me like so many others had. I had learned to strengthen my resolve and keep a tight leash on my emotions. I was fragile in every way except one. No one would break my heart again. I'd do whatever it took to stop that from happening.

Chapter 6

The icy air crawled against my skin as my horse trotted along, following the others. It stung my lungs in the best way possible. I loved the cold. The trees were missing half of their orange and yellow leaves, the weakest ones mixing with the muddy ground. The autumn had been unusually rainy for this part of Kinzlea, making the air wet and cold. The northern part of the kingdom was typically dry most of the year, but it was as if the clouds thought the ground needed more life.

I pulled my coat tighter around me, but even with the thick wool and the layer of fat on my body, the wind cut through my soul, making me shiver. I relished the cold weather, even as my body protested. It woke my senses, keeping my mind sharp.

Aukina wore a thin shirt, her mermaid blood keeping her more than warm enough. Between her physiology and the demon lover wrapped around her back, she was thriving in the chilled weather. Nyri was bundled up to her neck, but her eyes were bright with wonder, even as her nose was red. The only one who looked miserable was Satella, which made no sense.

The healer was a vampire, which meant the cold shouldn't have affected her. Yet, she hadn't stopped grumbling about her aching joints.

The trail of guards behind us said nothing as they followed. They were trained to withstand the cold—many of them responsible for watching over the estate at night in the dead of winter. I should've known better that it wasn't only going to be this small group of friends. Zathrian was protective of his mate. He wouldn't let her get into a situation that put her in harm's way. Nyri had merely smiled and greeted the group of trained warriors who met us by the stables in the morning.

Either she put up with her overprotective lover's orders to appease him, or she no longer felt safe after the multiple attacks on her life and relished the extra protection.

I shook my head. I could never love a demon king. The amount of pressure attached to someone like that wasn't worth it.

By the time we made it to the lake, my legs ached from the horse ride. I barely remembered the last time I had ridden a beast, but my body hated me for the journey.

Reamann helped Aukina off her horse before helping Nyri. I ignored the craving for a male to help me off the saddle. I didn't need anyone to help me. Not when I had my magic. I twisted off my horse and floated gently to my feet. I waved my hand and the reins tied themselves to the tree. Small uses of magic didn't wear on my body the same way as major bursts, so I was able to get away with it without consequences.

I pulled a carrot from my bag and held it out. "Thank you for carrying me, Tatzy." The horse huffed, shoving my hand away and making me drop the carrot. I pursed my lips, trying not to take it personally, but most animals didn't seem to like me.

I turned to the lake as the others unpacked their stuff and settled in. The extra guardsmen disappeared into the forest, likely scoping for any dangers. I hoped they'd stay out of sight, because the thought of being around that many people made me uncomfortable.

"Beautiful, isn't it?" Aukina asked. Her hair was tied into a braid that ended near her lower back. She was a little taller than me, and she was one of the curvier residents at Ethlow. She held her weight better than I ever had. She had proper curves, while I was just round. It was no wonder she was able to get someone as handsome as the orange-haired guardsmen.

"This is it?" I asked. I had expected a grand lake with clear waters after spending hours on a horse to get here.

Aukina rubbed the back of her neck. "I know it's not much, especially not compared to the sea, but it's nice to get away from the estate for a day. It's easy to stay locked indoors all the time at Ethlow. It can make you feel like a prisoner, instead of someone who's there by choice."

I bit my inner cheek, realizing my statement was harsher than I had intended. I didn't mean to insult Aukina's lake. It simply wasn't impressive.

"I like staying inside," I said. "It's safe inside. Most of the residents leave you alone, and then I don't have anyone telling me I'm an abomination or hunting me down because of my witchiness."

I felt Aukina's eyes shift to me, but I refused to look at her. I didn't want her pity.

The mermaid stroked the end of her braid, unable to look away. "I thought magic was common on land. I would have expected humans to appreciate a witch, especially one that was human."

"Some villages do," I said, carefully choosing my words. "But there are many who fear magic of any kind because of the Great Demon War. Magic slaughtered a lot of innocents who didn't have powers to protect themselves. Many humans decided to live in villages without magic, thinking they were better off without it."

"In the Hallow Sea, I was warned against demons. Most sea dwellers think that demons are all bad because of that war. But we understand that magic and demons are different." The mermaid's eyes slid to Reamann and sparkled. "It's a shame though. Many don't understand that being a demon doesn't make a being inherently bad. Just as being an elf doesn't make someone good."

"There are bad demons out there, though." I had come across more than my fair share of evil in my time. It was found in every shape and form one could think of.

"It's always the few that ruin it for everyone." Aukina's fingers curled until her knuckles turned white. She returned her attention back to the lake.

"It's because a demon's magic is stronger when they make deals with others. The more deals they have, the stronger they become.

Any being who needs others to be stronger is automatically villainized, just like vampires." Satella's eyes drifted over to us, confirming she had been listening to every word we said. I didn't blame her. If I had the senses and body of a vampire, I would've used them all the time.

"It doesn't make them evil though." Aukina huffed, her temper rising. She was usually sweet and smiling, but it was nice to see a tougher side to her. When it came to the demon she loved, she grew a backbone. It was strange seeing love strengthen someone instead of sucking the life out of them.

"No, it doesn't," I easily agreed. "Have you ever made a deal with a demon?"

Aukina scrunched her brows together. "No."

"Not even with Reamann?"

The mermaid shook her head. "He's never asked. I don't think he's ever made a deal with anyone."

"That's why he's weak, then." When Aukina turned her glare towards me, I quickly added, "For a demon." I wasn't sure if it helped ease my comment. I wasn't trying to insult Reamann. It was a fact that he was a lower demon, but most demons had the ability to gain power if they were smart enough to trick others into giving them their lifeforce.

Reamann cursed under his breath as he attempted to light wood in the center of a fire pit. Aukina looked grateful for the distraction, and my chest twinged. I didn't understand why I didn't know how to talk to others properly. It was as if my brain didn't process that there should've been a filter on my mouth until the words had come out.

I stalked after the mermaid, curious as to what was causing the demon issues.

"The air is wet, so it's taking longer to light," Reamann said. He struck the flint repeatedly, but the logs were damp and not taking the spark. A simple oversight.

I almost said as much, but for once, my filter worked. I flicked my hand as Reamann struck the flint, and the fire roared to life.

"Finally," Satella muttered. "I thought I was going to freeze because of your incompetence."

"You could have done it yourself," Reamann snapped.

Satella waved her hands. "I didn't want to break one of my nails."

"I didn't realize you were such a dainty princess."

Satella held up her middle finger and stared at the demon with no remorse. Those two acted as if they hated each other, but I had seen them laughing and smiling, so they couldn't have despised each other.

Aukina stepped in before the bickering continued, pulling Reamann towards the lake. He happily obliged, a puppy dog trailing the love of his life. Satella settled on a log, holding her hands out to the fire.

"Thank you," Nyri said. I hadn't realized she moved next to me. She was surprisingly silent for being in a forest filled with sticks and twigs. Maybe it was her magic's attunement to nature that made her move with ease, or maybe it was from years of trying to make herself look invisible.

"For what?" I blinked at the girl. We looked about the same age, but centuries weighed my shoulders down. We were at the opposite ends of the spectrum of life.

"For the fire." She kept her voice low, as if to keep the others out of the conversation.

"I don't know what you're talking about." I didn't like bringing attention to myself, even if I liked the praise.

"I felt your magic surge right before the fire sparked." Anyone who was paying attention could have sensed my magic in that moment, but it was easier for other magic wielders to feel the powers. "I've been paying attention, since you told me all magic has a personality."

"Good." I tugged at the tips of my fingers as I searched my brain for something else to say.

"So I've been thinking," Nyri started. I was grateful she took control of the conversation. "I think we should work together to make healing potions."

"Why?"

"Because you saved my life." It was only a few weeks ago that Nyri was bedridden on the verge of death. The healing tonic I had made brought her back from the brink of falling into the grasp of the underworld. As far as I knew, the tonic I made was the first of its kind. "And I think danger is coming to the estate."

Her last comment made me hesitate. Ever since Nyri's arrival at Ethlow, the energy of the estate had shifted. It was as if love had blossomed in disgusting waves, and everyone was finding a lover to hold at night. Ever since the demon king found love, the weight on the estate had lightened. It was better than the decades he spent mourning his lost love.

But the shadows grew darker, lingering in wait to consume the light that had brought smiles to everyone around me.

"Why?" I had felt the shift, but I didn't know the source yet.

Nyri shrugged. "Zathrian won't say anything. I think he's being overprotective, especially with what has happened recently, but he's coming back with bruises and cuts more frequently. I can see the worry in his eyes. I don't know what's going on, but I know I want to help him."

Nyri was a good match for the demon king, which was a strange thought. I had always thought someone powerful needed an equal. Nyri was in no way the demon king's equal, but she was kind and caring. A king that had to deal with darkness daily needed someone soft to take the edge away.

Maybe if I helped others like she did, others would like me more. Saving Nyri's life brought me closer to this friend group. If I agreed to work with Nyri, if I made myself more valuable to the estate, maybe I would become someone important to them. "I'll help you."

Chapter 7

Aukina jumped into the lake stark naked, the icy water splashing onto us. Reamann shouted, jumping back. He got the worst of the splash, since he had been trying to hide his lover's naked body from the guards watching over us. Aukina hadn't cared that others were around as she stripped down in preparation for her mermaid transformation. I couldn't understand her bodily freedom. I hated the thought of being naked in front of others.

"You should join me," Aukina called out. Her hair floated on the surface of the water, covering her breasts.

Reamann glanced around. "It's cold."

"I'll warm you up." Her wink made Reamann blush.

"Gross," I muttered under my breath.

"You'll understand when you find someone you like," Nyri chuckled.

Before I could tell her that wouldn't happen, Satella spoke. "No, I agree. Those two are grossly in love."

The laugh that escaped my mouth was louder than I intended. Reamann pulled his shirt off and tossed it to the side. His muscles rippled with the movement, and I found myself watching him a little too closely as he stripped his pants. The demon was a fine specimen, and I couldn't stop the ache from pooling between my legs. I'd never pursue another's lover, but it reminded me of my hidden desires that craved physical affection, the part of me that I tried to suppress.

I didn't need anyone else to scratch that itch.

At least that was what I told myself.

"You're grossly in love, too," Nyri cooed, looking at the vampire.

Satella narrowed her eyes. "Shut up."

Nyri chuckled, knowing she had won.

I wanted to join in the banter, but it was hard when my chest felt hollow. Every one of them was younger than me, yet they had found a love like I never had. I wasn't sure if it was jealousy or resentment, but I shoved the feelings down. I didn't want anyone to see the ugly thoughts in my head.

"I'm going to take a walk," I said.

"Want me to come with you," Nyri asked.

I smiled, appreciating the offer, but I didn't want her company. "No, I have to, um." I looked around. "Relieve myself."

Nyri's eyes widened. "Oh, yes. Just shout if you need anything. Someone should hear you."

I gave her a quick nod before stalking off into the forest alone. Animals skittered into hiding as they heard my footsteps approach. I lifted my skirt as I walked, but dead leaves and dirt clung to the fabric despite my best efforts. I kept walking until I was sure no one would overhear me before relieving myself as quickly as possible.

When I was done, I didn't rush back to the others. Wind rustled the remaining leaves on the trees, ripping off some with its invisible power. Clouds covered the sky, dark and ready for rain. We wouldn't have much longer until we needed to head back to the estate.

Zathrian allowed anyone who asked for refuge to stay at Ethlow as long as we followed the two rules set in place. The first was to do our part in upkeeping the estate. There were too many of us for anyone to live without working. Everyone had a role, whether it was cook, healer, or gardener. The other rule was to be inside the walls before dark. It was all about the safety of the residents. The veil between the underworld and the mortal realm grew weak at night, and there were times creatures from the underworld slipped into the mortal realm using the shadows.

It was easy for me to follow the second rule. I didn't leave the library often, and when I did, it was to visit the mess hall for food, get supplies, or see Satella for treatment.

I took in a slow breath, the cool air stinging my lungs, but it felt good compared to the other times of the year. Spring was the worst. The pollen made my lungs struggle more than usual. Summer wasn't much better.

I looked up at the clouds, wondering if the rain would drive us back to the estate early. I wouldn't have complained. It was nice being outside, but I wasn't sure how many more conversations I could muddle through.

The smell of snow brushed my nose, but it wasn't cold enough for that. It would be weeks, if not months, before snow came to

Ethlow. I wasn't surprised when a burst of heat licked the back of my neck. I looked at the closest tree, suddenly very interested in the gray pattern on the trunk.

"Are you stalking me?" I chewed on my lip, refusing to turn around. Despite my pounding heart, I wanted to seem as aloof as possible.

"If that's what it takes to get you to give in to me, I'll stalk you across the world." Jathral's voice was deep in my ear, sending a shiver down my spine. "Might as well give in to me now." His finger twisted around one of my curls, and the slight tug sent a shiver down my spine.

"You know what I want." My voice was quiet, but it was loud in the still air of the forest.

Jathral's hot breath brushed against the back of my neck, countering the cold. I liked the cold, but something about his warmth made me want to take it all in and devour him until there was nothing left.

"Yes," he purred, the rumble from his chest going straight to my core. "You want me on my knees before you." He dropped my curl and ran his fingers down my spine. I had to tighten every muscle to stop my body from physically reacting, but his chuckle in my ear begged me to stop resisting.

"Yet, here you are, not a single apology on your lips." My voice was shaky, but I pushed through it. I would *not* yield to Jathral. He thought he was better than me, better than everyone else. It was my personal mission to make him realize he was nothing but an arrogant bastard. He didn't deserve his title as king.

"I told you I don't apologize."

"Then fuck off." I debated about using my magic to push him away, force him onto his knees, but it was too risky out here. There were too many people that could ask the wrong questions. Perhaps that was why Jathral followed us out of the estate. Maybe he knew I was powerless without my library surrounding me.

"I've been thinking. We could make a compromise. You want me on my knees?" His fingers ran down my side, tracing my curves. My muscles tightened where he touched, and I couldn't control the visceral reaction any longer.

"Yes," I breathed, losing my confidence. I gritted my teeth, reminding myself of who stood behind me.

"Then maybe for you, for access to the library, I'll get on my knees." His voice was low and husky, and I didn't understand what he was saying.

I started to turn around. "What—"

He grabbed my hips, stopping me from turning towards him. He pushed on my spine, forcing me to bend forward. I caught myself against the tree, the bark stinging my hands. Magic swirled in my chest, ready to defend myself in whatever way necessary. I knew I couldn't physically take the demon king, but maybe magically I stood a chance.

I leashed my magic, a small spark of curiosity running through me as Jathral ran his fingers down the sides of my thighs.

Goddess, it had been too long since someone touched me like that.

The ground crunched behind me, and the looming presence sank. I couldn't see Jathral from that angle, but I felt the shift. He was on his knees, but when I tried to look at him again, he grabbed my hips, stopping me from moving.

"Here's how this is going to work," Jathral said, sliding his fingers under my skirt. "I will be on my knees for you, but it won't be an apology on my lips." The pads of his fingers barely brushed my skin, moving up and up and—

I hissed as he pressed against my inner thighs, making me step apart to spread my legs for him. I should've stopped him. Logically, I knew that. But as he moved even higher, a fire that had been dormant for too long ignited.

Jathral, the demon king of Mithcourt, was on his knees for *me*, ready to—

My mind went blank as he hooked his fingers around my undergarments and pulled them down, exposing my heat to the cool air. It didn't last long. As his tongue found my pussy, his warmth made my entire body jolt. I arched my back as he plunged deeper. I panted heavily, excitement filling my veins.

Jathral wasn't someone who would go for a witch like me. He was devilishly handsome and one of the five most powerful rulers in the lands. If it weren't for his attitude, he could get anyone he wanted. Even with his attitude, most would fall over themselves to get a taste of his powers.

But me, a lowly librarian witch, was someone he was willing to get on his knees for. I wasn't foolish enough to think that it was anything other than a bribe, but as he pushed his tongue deeper,

I didn't care. It had been too long since I had been touched like that, and I wasn't about to make him stop, not when his dexterous fingers swirled around my swelling bud.

A thrill went through my spine, and I arched harder, giving him better access. Jathral gripped my thighs, digging his fingers into my skin so hard I knew there would be bruises there later, but I didn't care. Not as my body tightened. Not as he pushed his tongue deeper, coaxing pleasure from deep within me.

An explosion from within erupted, making my vision go white briefly. Jathral continued lapping me up until I was drained of energy. I struggled to catch my breath, my fingers grasping the tree bark. Pain ebbed from my palm, and red stained the tree. I didn't know when the cut happened other than it was during the little escapade.

I forced myself to straighten, my body crying against my weakened muscles. I turned to face Jathral, unsure of what I'd say to him, but it didn't matter. I was alone in the forest. If it weren't for the slickness between my legs, I would have thought I had hallucinated the interaction. It had happened so fast, ending just as quickly.

That bastard didn't even say goodbye.

Chapter 8

I flexed my hand, testing the pain as I wandered through the bookshelves, searching for the section about elven history. Satella had wrapped my hand while giving me a lecture on my clumsiness. I took the warnings in silence, not wanting to tell her the details of how I got the cut. Part of me questioned if Jathral had actually shown up in the forest or if it was some sort of strange fantasy.

It didn't make sense. I wouldn't have imagined the asshole king doing something like that. I wanted to crush his arrogance. I didn't want his head between my thighs.

Even as I tried to tell myself that, I couldn't quell the pulse between my legs.

He had been on his knees. It wasn't an apology, but it was part of my stipulation.

I bit my lip to halt that line of thinking. The more I thought about the demon king of Mithcourt, the more power I gave him.

"Can you stop hiding my books from me?" I demanded, turning my attention back to the library. It had never hidden a section I wanted from me for more than a day, but it was going on over a week. I hadn't done anything to insult the world of knowledge—as far as I knew.

The shelves rumbled next to me. Now the library was sassing me.

"Very funny." My voice was dry. If the library didn't sense my irritation, it was as naive as I was when it came to others' emotions.

Pages fluttered in the distance, sounding like a cackle.

I didn't hide my sneer as I stormed off to find something else to do. Nyri wanted me to work with her to create potions with her special flowers. I had done it once, saving her life with a miracle, but replicating potions wasn't easy. I needed to learn everything I could about the flowers, but there was limited knowledge in my library. The best way to learn more about the magic the flowers held was to go to the island they originated from, but that would require talking to the island dwellers.

I wasn't good at talking to new people.

I pressed the tips of my fingers together as my frustration built. That was enough for the day. It was easier when I had been alone in my library. I didn't have a demon king harassing me for access to the library or others relying on me to make healing potions.

I reached the door to my private room when the air sizzled with power. The source of the magic was painfully familiar. I redirected my walk without thinking. As I reached the edge of the bookshelves, I slowed, being careful to stay behind the wards I had placed, especially when I took in Jathral's demeanor. His jaw clenched tight, and orange flames danced among the purple in his irises. His power surged when he saw me.

If I had thought he was moody before, I was wrong. His magic pressed against the wards, looking for an opening, but he would find none.

When he sensed my presence, his eyes settled on me, a surge of hate slammed against me. It took all my physical strength to hold my ground. I would not retreat from the bastard king just because he was angry.

"Why don't I have access to the library?" He hurled another blast of power against the invisible shield separating us. The ground shook under the power, but he would not break my wards. I had limited use of my magic due to my physical limitations, but I knew exactly how strong my powers were. Centuries of weaving protection spells had made mine the most powerful I had ever come across.

I looked him up and down, carefully inspecting his body. He was covered nearly head to toe in cloth, but it didn't stop his muscles from bulging through the thin fabric. It didn't hide the V-shape of his torso or his strong hips and thighs.

"Why would you have access?" I tilted my head slightly, which only pissed him off more.

A muscle in his jaw ticked, and it took him a moment to respond. "Because I got on my knees for you. I pleasured you." He said it matter-of-factly, as if those small gestures were enough to win my favor.

"I do not trade sexual acts for favors." I held firm, refusing to acknowledge the ache in my core as memories of his tongue between my thighs assaulted me. My gaze shifted to his hair, wondering what it'd be like to run my fingers through the black locks as he ate me out. Grabbing his horns would be even better, giving me control over the way he moved while between my thick thighs.

"I told you I'd get on my knees for you in exchange for access to the Ethlow library." His lip curled back, revealing his sharp teeth.

"I never agreed to that." It was a simple fact, one that made flames dance off Jathral's shoulders. "As a demon, you should know better than anyone else that for a deal to be valid, you have to have consent from both parties."

Jathral stepped forward, his claws and wings out. Despite his handsome facade, the demon in front of me would terrify those not accustomed to demons and other monsters.

"What will it take for you to give me access to the library? Do I need to fuck you into submission?"

There was something about the demon's words that made my core ache. If he was skilled with his fingers and tongue, I wondered what he could do with the package that was obvious under his pants.

"I've already told you what you need to do. Apologize, and then I'll consider letting you step foot beyond this shield." My heart thundered, but not in fear. Knowing I had full control sent a jolt through my spine that only made my core ache more.

His rage flared, but then he steeled himself, hardening his expression. "I don't apologize."

"Okay." I turned to leave. I wasn't going to give in to the demon's whims because he was angry.

"Don't you dare walk away from me." The roar of flames filled my ears before heat hit my back. His magic couldn't hit me directly, but he could make the room boil from his sweltering fire magic.

I spun on my heels, my magic pulling up freezing temperatures from deep within me, ready to douse the fire-wielding demon in ice. The flames were contained to his fists, so I kept my magic in my chest, making it squeeze my lungs.

"If you try to set this place on fire, I will kill you." No one threatened my library.

"That'd be impossible, even if you were brave enough to try." The taunt in his voice made my magic flare. His complete arrogance and doubt of my abilities struck a blow to me. He was no different than the humans who destroyed me.

I stepped forward, ice crusting the tips of my fingers. "Don't underestimate me." The crackle within me begged me to use my magic to overpower him. It wanted to destroy the demon king to prove him wrong. It didn't care about the consequences that would come with using that much power.

Jathral took his time scanning every inch of my body. Despite the distance and ward between us, it felt as if his fire was caressing my skin with the way my body burned. "I see right through you, witch. You are so desperate to prove that you're strong that you think you can fight someone more powerful than you. If you keep that attitude, you're going to get yourself killed."

His words were a blow to my stomach. My magic threatened to release without control to prove the asshole wrong. Three strangled breaths hit my lungs. That was how long it took to leash my powers.

"You're not worth my energy." My neck burned as my magic said otherwise. It whispered beneath my skin, desperate for me to let go of control.

I forced myself to walk away, turning my back on the demon king. My legs threatened to shake with each step.

Jathral snarled at my indignation. He moved forward, the wards warning me even as I kept my eyes off the demon king. A second later, electricity snapped into the air. Jathral hissed, and I glanced over my shoulder. He was relatively unharmed, but his hand was singed from where he tried to break through the wards.

I won this battle, but it was the beginning of a war.

Chapter 9

I was amazed by the rows of bleeding heart lilies filling the greenhouse. The flower was rare, especially in Kinzlea where the air was dry and often frigid. The delicate flowers bloomed best in warm and humid environments, which the greenhouse simulated perfectly between the glass structure and the demon king's magic that weaved throughout the building. The true reason the flowers thrived was because of the human standing next to me.

"There's a lot of bleeding heart lilies." I counted two dozen fully grown flowers, but there were more seedlings in the back row.

"Yeah, but I haven't been able to get another purple variant." Nyri pursed her lips, twisting a strand of her hair between her fingers.

Bleeding heart lilies were known for their white petals and red core that looked like blood, but there were records of a purple variant with gold filaments instead of red. I had thought they were a myth until the young witch had made one blossom over the summer.

"How did you do it before?" I touched one of the flowers, feeling its delicate magic pulse through me. It was a fragile magic, which was why the flowers struggled to grow under regular conditions.

They needed someone who could stoke their powers and put more than the basics into tending them.

The young witch didn't understand this. It was clear from her furrowed brows. She knew how to tend to the flowers, but it was her pure heart that made them thrive.

Nyri shook her head. "I don't know. Aukina said the people of the Nescen Islands tell stories about true love cultivating the purple variant, but we didn't do anything special when the flower bloomed."

I scoffed. "True love is a thing of fairy tales."

Nyri bit her lip and looked away. "Maybe it was a fluke."

Too harsh. I understood that, yet I didn't have the words to comfort her—not when I meant what I said. I knew she thought she loved the demon king, but their passion would burn out eventually. Attraction faded and hearts grew apart. It was the natural way of life, especially for the beings who lived for centuries.

"It wasn't a fluke." I had seen the purple flower. The flower's magic was different than the others. It was why I had chosen that flower to make the healing potion. I wished I had had time to study it before destroying it.

"Then how did it change?" Nyri asked. It was a great question. One I didn't know the answer to.

I reached out with my magic, searching the flower for any information about the magic itself. The flower twisted around the energy I sent into it until it yielded, revealing a core of untouched power. I tried to push further, but the flower recoiled. It didn't like my magic, which shouldn't have been a surprise. It didn't stop the tightness in my chest from taking over.

"Something needs to awaken it," I announced. My magic wasn't the right flavor, but neither was Nyri's regular magic.

"Like what?"

I didn't have the answer. I pulled at my fingers, searching my knowledge for something, anything that would help, but I drew a blank.

"Try doing what you did before." I was sure Nyri had thought of that, but if I witnessed her magic, maybe it'd help me understand what she was doing wrong.

"I didn't do anything special that time," Nyri answered. "I was just showing the others the flowers blooming, and one of them changed colors."

So the key was in the moment the flowers bloomed. "Show me."

Nyri approached a row of flower buds, ready to ripen. A single touch was all it took for the flower to grow and the petals unfurl. Tendrils of red rained down from the center as if the flower was bleeding. It was no wonder why the obsession with them was so great. Even if the regular population didn't understand the true magic of the flower, they felt it. It drove the price of the flower to levels only nobles could afford, even if the flower had been dried and preserved.

"It's still white." Nyri's shoulders sank as she pressed her lips into a tight line.

"I know." As Nyri's magic stroked the flower, there wasn't anything unusual about it or the flower. "Maybe try thinking about love when you do the next one." I hated saying that. It was difficult to imagine love being a true factor.

Nyri nodded. She closed her eyes, and her face brightened as she likely thought about Zathrian. A twinge tugged at my diaphragm, but I ignored it, probing Nyri's magic as she touched the next flower. Her magic was warmer, but the flower didn't react differently. I was right. True love wasn't enough to change the flower's magic core, which meant it had been something else.

"Shame," I said. "We'll figure it out." It wasn't a fluke. I didn't believe in those when it came to magic. I understood how magic took and fed on the world, how it gave back to nature, how it could create and destroy.

Nyri didn't look as confident. Failure weighed in her eyes. She wanted to help. She wanted to be an asset to the demon king she fell in love with, but she didn't know how.

"We'll figure it out," I repeated, this time with a smile. I didn't have confidence in Aukina's theory behind the purple flower, but I had confidence in Nyri. Despite her being a young witch, her magic breathed life into the world around her. It was a gift that she could do worlds of good with once she mastered it. I was determined to help her do just that. I wanted to be able to say I trained one of the greatest witches of the century, and I knew she had the power within her to reach that status.

Love and Magic, the Fables of Fate and Emotion in Witches.

I studied the book title with a grimace. "This you find me, but you won't let me read about elven history." I sneered in no particular direction, knowing the walls felt my irritation. It was the one place I felt like I could be myself. I didn't have to dance around the emotions of others or worry about saying the wrong thing. If I was in a bad mood, I could show it, and the library didn't treat me differently.

I grabbed the book with a huff. It felt like a taunt, as if the library wanted to tell me I was foolish to not believe in love. Maybe the book would have important information in it. Even if true love didn't exist, emotions affected a witch's powers. There was no denying that.

Meow. Binx's soft pur came from the front of the library. It was strange for him to be out of my room. He was even more of a recluse than me. I followed the sounds to the front desk where Binx sat, leaning into Viridian's touch. I lifted an eyebrow, surprised by the sight.

"Binx doesn't like people."

The demon's eyes flashed teal, and his lips lifted. Not quite a smile, but as close as I had ever seen the master of the house get. "I don't like people. Guess we have that in common."

A low pur flowed from Binx as he shoved his head against the demon's palm. It was a strange sight to see the two get along.

"Same."

Viridian turned to me, but he kept his hand on my cat's head. "You like people. You're just afraid of getting hurt, so you tend to stay away from them."

I swallowed hard. I didn't appreciate the accusation, but I didn't have an argument against his statement. Instead, I changed the subject. "If you're here about Jathral, then you're wasting your time. Until he apologizes, I won't remove the wards against him."

"That is never going to happen. I have never seen the king of Mithcourt apologize for anything." Viridian dropped his hand, but Binx didn't appreciate it. He moved to rub against the demon's perfectly ironed black vest.

"Then I suppose he will never get what he wants." That thought pleased me more than it should've. Jathral was the type to bully others into getting his way.

"In different circumstances, I would tell you to hold out." The exception lingered on his tongue, but he didn't have to say more to make it obvious what was on his mind.

"You're the one who told me to make it difficult for him." I tightened my grip on the book in my hands. Viridian couldn't order me to give Jathral access, and the look in his eyes told me he knew that.

"Difficult, not impossible."

I huffed, my body heating with annoyance. "All he has to do is apologize. That's not an impossible task."

"For him, it is." Viridian likely knew Jathral better than most. They had been through the Great Demon War together and had lived in the same world nearly a millennium since.

"That's not my problem. If he's too arrogant to admit his own flaws, then the asshole can suffer." I felt no sympathy for the demon king. Not when he damaged my library and hurt Nyri.

"Normally, I would agree, but unfortunately, he saved my life recently. He's calling in the favor." Shadows danced on Viridian's shoulders, reflecting the frustration he felt.

"Once again, I fail to see how that's my problem. He's calling in a favor from you. Not me."

Viridian didn't blink. "I'm well aware of that, Tareen." The way he said my name sent a shiver down my spine, and not the good kind. "I am here to make a deal with you. If you give Jathral access to the library, then I will owe you a favor that you may recall at a later time of your choosing."

This caught my attention. A favor from the great Shadow Slinger was a powerful tool to have. "What are the limitations of the favor?" I knew better than to simply accept a deal from a demon without questions. I learned that the difficult way.

"The favor cannot bring harm to King Zathrian or his lover."

I cocked my eyebrow. I hadn't expected him to include Nyri in that protection, not that I intended to ever bring harm to her. "Anything else?"

"No." A simple but powerful deal.

I'd have been a fool to reject it. I reached my hand out. "Deal."

Viridian's face was as still as stone as he pulled off his glove. "Deal."

He scratched my palm with his claw, slicing through the skin as if it was made of cobwebs. Blood leaked onto his finger, and his powers surged, moving through my veins. His shadows burned into the palm of my hand, leaving behind a signet in the shape of a black bat that looked as if it was dripping. My skin burned with the remnants of the demon's power.

Viridian's eyes shifted to the book in my arms. He lifted his brows. "I didn't take you for someone interested in that subject." He acted as if we hadn't made a deal that granted me anything I wished for.

Heat crawled up my neck. "I'm not," I snapped. Viridian was one of the few beings who didn't treat me differently for being myself. "I'm doing research to help Nyri."

Viridian hummed, his lack of words making me feel self-conscious.

"Is that all?" I asked, my tone clipped.

"For now." Viridian stepped back, shadows devouring him until I was alone with Binx.

I looked at my palm. The power felt different than the other signet on my abdomen. This was a deal that was in my favor. It was rare for a demon to make that kind of deal. Whatever Jathral needed from my library was more important than I had imagined if Viridian had been willing to get involved.

Chapter
10

I t was only a matter of time for Jathral to show up, but as days passed by, I was surprised by the demon's absence. With his prior anger and desperation, I had prepared for him to visit the library the moment Viridian left.

On the third day after the master of the house left his mark on me, the power in the library shifted. Binx meowed, dashing off into the shadows. I shut my book before standing, but I didn't have to go anywhere before flames appeared in front of me, dangerously close to a bookshelf. I quickly wondered if it was a mistake to make a bargain with Viridian.

Jathral's power filled my throat, and he stood in front of me, a cocky grin painting his lips. I wanted to smack his face until he learned he wasn't better than me.

It was definitely a mistake to let that asshole back into my library.

"Before you touch anything, there are rules you should know. If you break any of them, I will revoke your privileges." My hand burned, a warning against going back on my deal with the demon. "If you burn or damage the books in any way, I won't hesitate to kick you out without a chance to come back. You are not to bother me with stupid questions."

Jathral took a step forward, heat lingering on his body from his fire magic. "What if I bothered you with other activities?" He smirked, a dangerous glee moving through his face.

I clenched my thighs at the memory of his tongue between my legs. I hated the ache in my core that followed, the soft pulse between my legs.

I pushed past Jathral, hanging onto my hatred for him. Just because he was skilled with his tongue, it didn't mean I had to give into those primal desires. "I told you, I don't trade sexual favors. Follow the rules, and I won't have to kill you."

His footsteps rang loudly behind me. The hardwood floors made it easy to track the demon behind me, but something told me I would know exactly where he was even if he followed me silently.

"I already have access to the library. This doesn't have to mean anything. Just two beings indulging in carnal pleasure." His deep voice flowed around me, caressing my ears.

He was messing with me. There was no other explanation for why a demon king would want me. I spun on my heels, but Jathral didn't stop until his body was nearly pressed against mine. "What game are you playing?"

Jathral stepped forward, his eyes darkening. I stepped back until my back was pressed against the wall. The demon towered over me, and the fresh scent of snow filled my nostrils, promising a new beginning.

"I'm not playing games. You enjoyed my mouth on you in the forest. I thought you'd enjoy it again." He leaned down until his lips were inches above mine.

I wondered what he would taste like. Would he be sweet like the scent of winter berries that clung to him? Or would he be bitter like his personality? With a shaky breath, I pushed that thought away.

"I would never sink that low." I kept my voice taut. I didn't want him to hear the moment of hesitation.

He moved closer to my neck and inhaled slowly. My muscles tensed, his proximity sending a tingle down my spine.

"I can smell your arousal. You can't hide your thoughts from me." His nose brushed against my neck, making me lose my sense briefly.

I hated my body for betraying me. Jathral was beyond attractive, and my fingers wanted to roam his muscles, to feel the hardness beneath my soft fingers. But doing anything with the demon king would have been a colossal mistake.

I pushed against his sculpted chest, pushing down any drop of temptation. "There is only one way I'd ever do anything with you again, and it would require you to be beneath me, begging for more."

I surged my magic as I pushed Jathral, the force of it making him step back. I walked away, swaying my hips to show confidence I didn't feel. I had to get away from him before he saw how my lungs ached from the use of my magic. I felt the burn rising at an alarming rate. I hadn't used enough magic to trigger that kind of response, but something about Jathral made the side effect of my powers worse than usual.

"What if I said we could make that happen?" His voice was further away. He hadn't bothered to follow me that time.

"I'd call you a liar." My heart thundered, but I kept walking.

"Why?"

I stopped, hesitating as I reached my door. "Because you won't even apologize for destroying my library. You won't beg to be beneath someone else, especially not someone like me." My throat squeezed shut, barely able to sputter the last words.

I slipped into my room, refusing to give him the courtesy of a response. I slammed my back against the wall, knowing I was safe from the eyes of the demon within the confines of my room. He was allowed in the library, but there were several wards on my chambers, keeping everyone out, unless they received explicit permission from me.

My chest heaved up and down as I struggled to catch my breath. It didn't come from nerves. I wasn't scared of Jathral and what he could do to me. Or do for me. Anytime I used my powers with him, my magic had an adverse effect, worse than any other time I used it. Despite the amount I used being relatively small, my lungs ached, drained from the side effects of the power.

It should've been fine to use that much magic, but my chest tightened around my lungs in an all too familiar pain. I had to get to Satella if I wanted to avoid an attack that stopped my lungs altogether.

Binx meowed, rubbing against my leg.

I know. I know. I couldn't say the words out loud as I struggled to find my breath. I needed to get to the healer before it got worse, but if I left my room, I'd risk running into Jathral.

I counted my breaths, hoping I could quell the attack on my lungs on my own, but I couldn't take deep breaths. My vision started to darken at the edges, and this was not an attack I could push through. As much as I wondered what it'd be like to have the shadowed claws of the underworld drag me under for good, death scared me. I didn't want Jathral to see me like this, but dying was much worse.

Maybe he'd be off doing his own thing and wouldn't notice me.

I left my room, Binx at my heels. I moved slowly, careful not to aggravate my lungs further. I barely focused on my surroundings, only caring about getting to Satella. Binx hissed as footsteps approached from behind.

"Change your mind after all, witch?" Jathral purred from behind me.

I ignored him, stumbling forward. I clutched my desk, taking a moment to try to stabilize myself, but it didn't work.

"What's wrong with you?" His voice was harsh and demanding.

"Go. Away." I said between wheezes.

Jathral grabbed my arm. His voice lowered, his jaw tense. "*What* is wrong with you?"

I wanted to yell at him, to tell him to get off me, but I didn't have the breath to spare. "Lungs. Satella. Now."

I pushed off the table, knowing I had to keep moving. If I didn't make it to Satella soon, my lungs could give out. Part of me had felt invincible. I had survived centuries longer than what made sense. Even with my weak body, I thought the magic from the demon kept me alive, even if it was just barely, but as my vision grew darker, mortality filled my veins.

Jathral didn't release my arm. Instead, he scooped me against his chest, and flames erupted around us. The heat made sweat roll down the back of my neck, and the air disappeared from my lungs. The lack of oxygen increased the pressure in my chest, and my panic only made everything worse.

"What the fuck?" Satella shouted. "What did you do to her?"

"I'm saving her life," Jathral snarled.

"Put her down." Satella's voice was firm, her sweet voice nowhere in sight.

Jathral set me on the bed. "What's wrong with her?"

"None of your business, fuckhole," Satella snapped. "Now get out of my infirmary. I don't need you getting in the way."

Flames filled the air, and then Jathral was gone.

Chapter
II

My lungs ached, but with each moment that passed by with Satella's treatment, breathing had become easier. Tears pricked my eyes as fear refused to let go of my chest. I had become used to difficulties breathing, but it had never been that bad. Maybe my body had finally had enough of the demon's magic infused with it, and it was starting to burn out. Maybe this was the beginning of the end, and that thought scared me more than I thought it would have. I had thought when my time came, it'd be a relief.

I was wrong.

Satella watched me closely, her expression shifting from worry to anger. She clenched and unclenched her fists as she paced the room. Questions burned in her eyes, but she waited while I caught my breath. Speaking only made the ache in my throat worse.

"What the fuck happened?" Satella's resolve broke.

I flinched at the fury in her eyes. It felt as if I had messed up. "I had a breathing attack."

"I know that." Satella ran her fingers through her short black curls. "But why the fuck were you with Jathral?" She rarely cursed around me like that, so I knew I struck a nerve.

"It wasn't by choice." Venom coated my tongue as I thought about the demon king. I hated that he brought me to Satella and saved me when I could've handled it myself.

Satella lifted her brows, as if she didn't believe me. "I'm going to need more than that."

I took as deep of a breath as possible, taking in herb infused steam. That inhale threatened a coughing fit, but the steam fought my failing lungs. "Viridian asked me to let the asshole use my library. Something about a personal debt to Jathral."

Satella's face twisted, moving through a range of emotions. "I don't like him."

I huffed, which instantly caused me to cough. Once I got my lungs under control again, I said, "I don't either. I didn't want him to set foot in my library after what he did to it." I paused and then added, "And Nyri." I should've been more upset about what he did to a person than my library, but saying that would've been a lie. "But Viridian was very convincing." I curled my hand, hiding the mark on my palm.

Satella's eyes flicked to my hand, catching the subtle movement. "Be careful around demons. I know it's easy to let our guard down around them, but ones like Jathral will take advantage of you if you give him the chance."

Flashes of the rendezvous in the forest filled my head. I hadn't told the others about Jathral eating me out, partly because I hadn't been sure it was real, but also because I didn't want to admit I had let him continue because I enjoyed it.

"I know." My voice was quiet as my defenses rose. I knew exactly what kind of demon Jathral was, but I had given him access to my library for my own personal gains. I wanted to be mad at him, but he had helped me when I could barely breathe. I didn't know what to make of that, so I tucked it away somewhere to deal with later.

"I worry about you," Satella said. "You're always in that library alone. If you have a breathing attack and no one is around, it'd take too long for someone to find you."

"I'm fine." My walls slammed around my heart. If I let myself believe Satella truly cared, it'd hurt more later if she decided I wasn't worth a friendship. "I have stayed alive on my own for this long. I can take care of myself."

"*Jathral* carried you here, and your lips were already blue. As much as I hate the asshole, he saved your life. Tareen, you may like to think you don't need anyone, but I've been your healer for five decades. I have seen the decline in your health, and there's nothing I can do about it, especially when you act like you don't need anyone else. I don't know why your health is declining, but maybe if you met me halfway, we could figure out something to ease the symptoms. Only you can help you at this point, but you act like you've already given up."

I knew exactly why my lungs had weakened over the decades, but telling Satella the truth wouldn't do anything to fix me. Nothing and no one could fix my health, not when it was tied to the very demon that gave me my magic.

"Thank you for your help today, but I don't need you to worry about me." I forced myself to stand up, even though my legs shook.

It'd take several days for me to recover from this bout, but I would recover. The demon that held my soul would have no more use for me if I was dead. Or maybe that was exactly what he wanted. Then my soul would be his to wield for the rest of eternity.

I didn't go to lunch for the next several days, unable to get Satella's words out of my head.

You act like you've already given up.

She didn't understand that there was nothing I could do, even if I wanted to. My younger self was the one who made a deal with the worst kind of demon, and my older self was paying for it. The kind of magic I could wield was declining. The magic I used on Jathral shouldn't have caused that intense of a reaction.

I had barely used my powers since, afraid that any small thing would set it off. The last thing I needed was to cause another attack and find myself back in the infirmary with Satella's intense gaze searching for answers that didn't matter.

My lungs recovered as they always did, easing the panic that I had succumbed to. The demon I made the deal with needed me alive to siphon my life force. He'd be weaker with me dead. At least that was what I told myself to settle my nerves. It gave me the courage to step back onto the library floor, knowing very well who roamed the bookcases.

From my room, I had felt Jathral's magic surging through the library. It made me stay in bed an extra day. When I faced the arrogant demon, I needed the energy to fight back.

The library was quiet. I left my broom against the wall, knowing I wouldn't use it today. I wouldn't use it for several days to ensure I didn't fall back into a breathing attack from use of my magic. The room was void of Jathral's powers, which was a relief. I didn't want to face the fact that he had carried me to the infirmary. I didn't want to admit that his help might have made him a better demon than I had thought.

Jathral didn't want me to die, but that didn't make him less of an arrogant asshole who thought he could get whatever he wanted.

"Can I please get my book about elven history back?" I asked the bookshelves. Power rumbled in response.

No.

I pressed my lips together, unsure of what to do. The library had never been that stubborn before. I tried to figure out if there was something I had done to upset it, but letting Jathral into the walls was the only thing I could think of. That happened *after* the library decided to hide my research from me.

"I didn't take you as the type to say please."

I whipped my head around and saw Jathral leaning against a bookshelf. He crossed one leg over the other, and his elbows rested on a shelf behind him. He didn't use his fire magic to appear, which meant he had been there for longer than I realized. I scrunched my nose, annoyed that he was able to sneak up on me like that.

"I'm not in the mood for you today." I walked past the demon, unsure of where I was going. I didn't want to go back to my room, not after spending days locked inside.

"There's the attitude I'm used to." He followed closely, but his footsteps were silent behind me.

"What do you want?" My muscles tightened as I turned on the demon. I glared at him with the might of a warrior.

He looked me up and down, his gaze heating my skin. "Your lips aren't blue, and you're as feisty as ever. Good."

I blinked at him slowly. "Were you worried about me?" The words sounded ridiculous as they came out of my mouth. I was sure the demon king in front of me never cared about another soul in his entire life.

Jathral's eyes narrowed. "Not in the way you think. If you die, then I lose my source of information."

That made more sense. Jathral needed me. He didn't care about my life. "You have access to the library. What else could you possibly want with me?"

His gaze dropped to my lips. Power flashed through his eyes, sending a shiver down my spine. His smirk was laced with the arrogance the demon liked to flaunt. It made me want to destroy the smirk, to tear him down a few levels—especially knowing he likely thought I was weak after the breathing attack.

"I have access to your books, but I can't seem to find what I'm looking for. Since your library is as stubborn as you and likes to rearrange itself, it's your responsibility to find it for me." No please or thank you in his orders.

"No." I crossed my arms.

"I wasn't asking." Jathral stepped closer, his power surrounding me in a threat. My own power surged, begging me to use it against the demon, but I refused to succumb to the whims of my magic or the demands of the demon in front of me.

I grabbed the demon's tie and pulled him close to my face. "That's the problem with demons like you. You think you can order everyone around just because you fought in the Great Demon War. Well, guess what? Others fought and died for you to take the throne. You should be serving others in thanks, not taking advantage of those you deem beneath you. Someone should really put you in your place."

"And who would dare do something as stupid as that?" His eyes sparkled, a challenge dancing in them.

The smart thing to do was walk away. Pretending I didn't care would damage his pride, but I wasn't interested in pretending anything and looking weak. Not after Jathral had to carry me to the infirmary because my body didn't want to work.

"Me." I shoved against his chest until his back hit the nearest bookcase. His eyes widened in delicious surprise, and I knew I was going to enjoy this.

Chapter
12

"Do you honestly think you can handle me?" Jathral asked, quickly gathering himself.

"Stop talking. I'm tired of your voice." And his condescending nature. I was tired of everyone looking at me like I was frail.

"What are you going to do to stop me?" His lips curled into a smile, taunting me. He didn't think I would do anything, but I would prove him wrong.

I yanked his tie until his face was against mine. My mouth covered his, forcing him to stop talking. I nipped his lip, a threat and a promise of what I would do if he fought against me, but that wasn't an issue.

Jathral tasted like lemons and honey—nothing like I expected. I sucked his lip into my mouth before nipping it again. His fingers tangled in my curls as he deepened the kiss. He wanted more, but I wasn't about to give it to him.

I pulled back and looked into his swirling irises. Desire pooled there, eager for more. It was my turn to smirk. I was in control, and I was going to bring the man to the edge only to leave him wanting more.

My grip on his tie tightened as I dragged him to the closest table. He followed behind willingly—at least he didn't fight.

I let go of him and hopped onto the desk, using a smidge of magic to help me up. I couldn't afford to falter in front of Jathral, not when I was determined to show him I was anything but fragile.

"Get on your knees," I ordered.

"What makes you think—"

I grabbed his tie, pulling his face to eye level. My magic flared in my chest, begging me to unleash it on him, but I didn't need magic to put him in his place. "I said, get on your knees." I placed a gentle kiss against his lips, and the demon king fell to his knees.

Jathral looked up at me with a mix of anger and desire. He had gotten on his knees for me in the middle of the forest, but that was on his terms. This was on mine, and he hated every second of it. Yet, he followed my instructions anyway. If he didn't want to do this, he could have used his magic to whisk himself away in a burst of flames.

I grabbed his chin and leaned forward. "Be a good demon and show me how skilled that tongue of yours is."

Jathral curled his lips back, but he didn't argue. Instead, his hands went to my hips, and he pulled down my bottoms, leaving my lower half exposed to him. I held my breath, not daring to let my insecurities show. I couldn't let Jathral see me squirm under his gaze, afraid of what he might think of my thick thighs and scars. I couldn't show him any weakness, no matter how many rolled beneath the surface of my skin.

Jathral grabbed my knees, pulling my legs apart. A blast of heat stroked my inner thighs as his focus landed on the pink between my legs. Then his eyes roamed over my thighs, taking in the remnants of burn marks from ages ago. His entire body went taut at the sight. He hadn't seen the ruined flesh before, since my clothes hadn't come off in the forest.

My heart thundered, expecting him to call me ugly and scarred. Before he got the chance, I grabbed his horns and pulled his face between my thighs. The moment his lips pressed against my core, pleasure jolted my body. The demon swiped his tongue through my slit, and my breath hitched. It didn't take much coaxing for him to move his tongue as deftly as before.

His mouth was warm and wet against me, sending surges of pleasure running through my spine. I gripped his horns tighter, pulling him deeper. He groaned, and the vibrations made my body quiver. All thoughts of logic left my brain as pleasure filled every inch of me. I needed more. I needed the demon king to be inside of me until I used him to find my release.

I pushed his head down, guiding his mouth to exactly where I needed. He gripped my thighs, spreading my legs more as he swirled his tongue around my clit. Jathral was relentless with sucking, nipping, licking. It was as if his tongue had split in two to pleasure every part of me simultaneously.

I rolled my hips against his face in feverish delight. He pulled my body to the edge of the table with ease, despite my extra weight. It was as if I weighed nothing for his toned muscles. Breathless moans escaped my lips, barely audible as the demon explored my pussy, discovering exactly what made my body ache.

If I hadn't been holding onto his horns, I was sure I would've floated away from the ecstasy filling my veins.

Jathral plunged his tongue into my entrance while stroking my clit with a second tongue, and I lost it. My body clenched around him on the verge of coming undone. His tongue moved deeper than what should've been possible. It was as if the muscle had grown and expanded to reach the deepest part of me. His tongues coaxed the pleasure deep within me, and I couldn't hang on any longer.

I cried out, holding his head between my legs as the pressure released in waves and waves of euphoric pleasure. It left me completely breathless, but not like magic had. My lungs felt strong and steady with each breath, even as I struggled to gulp down enough air.

My hands slid off Jathral's horns, allowing him enough freedom to pull back and look up at me. His eyes sparkled with a light that didn't fit his brooding nature. His lips glistened with my arousal coating them.

It was a beautiful and damning sight. The arrogant demon king was on his knees to pleasure me. After feeling weak and helpless for the past few days, a new strength filled my veins.

I could get used to the image in front of me.

"It's much better when you don't use your tongue for talking," I said.

Jathral's face hardened. "Maybe we should test the same theory out on you."

"If you think I am ever going to get on my knees for you, then you are delusional."

Jathral's eyes darkened, but he kept his mouth shut. Then his eyes shifted to my thighs, looking at the burn marks. "What happened to you?"

My stomach twisted. I had wanted him to forget about the scars, but I had been too swept up in the moment to cover myself the moment we were done. I hopped off the table, gathering my bottoms and pulling them up as quickly as possible. "It's none of your business."

Letting myself be exposed in front of the demon king was a mistake, even if it had felt better than any human I had gotten into bed with.

"Did you burn yourself?" Jathral stood, towering over me. His power crept through the air, a reminder of his strength.

"No." My voice was terse. I hadn't said what had happened out loud before, even as it haunted my dreams. I preferred to suffer in silence.

"Then what happened?" Determination laced Jathral's face. He wasn't going to let this go easily.

"Why do you care?" I straightened my clothes, ready to walk away, but I hesitated.

"I don't." His voice was sharp, and I thought it was the end of the conversation. Then he said, "Those were deep burns. They didn't happen by accident."

I searched his eyes, looking for his thoughts. I couldn't read his face, other than a sliver of sincerity behind those powerful eyes.

"I was burned at the stake for being a witch." I didn't know why I decided to be honest, especially with Jathral of all demons, but in that moment, it felt safe to tell him the truth.

His face hardened, hiding his emotions. "By humans?" His voice was barely above a whisper. It was as if he spoke louder, he'd lose control.

I nodded, my throat turning dry at the memory. I wanted to turn away from the demon king. I wanted to go back to my room and hide from the world, but there was something about him that made me stand tall. I refused to show my weaknesses to him.

"This is why humans are inferior beings, and I don't let them live at Mithcourt." Pure hatred burned in his eyes.

A hatred that used to live deep in my heart.

"I've never been to Mithcourt," I said. "I haven't lived outside Kinzlea."

Jathral paused. "You're centuries old. You're the oldest one in Ethlow, aside from Zathrian and Viridian."

I shrugged. "Life outside these walls wasn't kind to me, and once I was here, I had no interest in leaving."

His gaze burned into my eyes, searching for answers I likely didn't have. "You're probably better off. The world is cruel. All humans deserve to die, and so do many other races."

I huffed, wondering if Jathral saw me as human. If he didn't, I wouldn't have blamed him. I was no longer human in the ways that mattered. "Not all humans are bad." I wasn't sure why those were the words I chose. There was a time I didn't believe that statement.

"Like you?" Such a simple question, but there was more behind the intention.

"No. In some ways, I'm just as bad as them, if not worse." To call myself innocent would have been an utter lie. Innocent humans didn't make deals with demons to destroy her enemies. They didn't watch the ones who burned her burn in return. "I'm thinking of Nyri. She has a good heart."

Jathral huffed. "Zathrian's consort?"

"Zathrian's chosen mate," I corrected. "The woman you tried to kill when you destroyed my library." Bitterness washed over my tongue, and I remembered exactly who I was talking to. Jathral didn't deserve the knowledge of my past, yet I had given it to him anyway, high on the pleasure of his tongue.

"I wasn't trying to kill the girl," Jathral said. He smoothed down his shirt, perfecting it again.

"And I think you're a good-hearted demon." Sarcasm dripped off my tongue.

Jathral smirked, and my core tightened. "I didn't think I'd ever hear those words from you, little mouse." His cocky grin made heat surge through my body. The desire to get on top of him and make him submit overwhelmed me, but I knew that was a dangerous line to tow.

"Don't get used to it, jackass." I walked away before my body betrayed me.

Chapter
13

I couldn't steady my heart as I walked to the courtyard where I knew Satella and the others were eating. It had been days since I had last seen them, and shame burned in my cheeks. Would they hate me for my absence? Would Satella brush me off for the way I ignored her concern?

Nyri's face brightened the moment I walked outside, and a weight fell off my shoulders. "You're feeling better!" She scrambled to her feet, leaving her dinner on the ground by the others. "I was getting worried about you."

I shrugged. *Worried.* Nyri had been worried, like Satella had been. It was a strange concept, having others to worry about me.

"I get sick a lot." I glanced at the vampire. She was stretched out in the sun, going against a vampire's natural instincts. She watched me carefully with a soft face. She didn't look angry, but she hadn't rushed to greet me like Nyri. "But I've been thinking. Maybe there's a way to fix my body so it's not so bad. If I strengthened my lungs, then maybe the breathing attacks would be less frequent."

I had come to the decision to ask for help after Jathral had left. For a moment, I had felt strong and young. It wasn't a feeling I remembered having before. Then I told him about my past, the day that made me throw everything away. Being honest had lifted a weight off my shoulders, but it had only been a brief respite.

Between the taste of ease and Satella's scolding, I didn't want to sit around accepting my broken body. I would never fix everything because of the bargain I had made, but maybe there was hope for a better life.

Satella's eyes lit up. "I think we can make that happen."

"Maybe the bleeding heart lilies can help," Nyri said.

"What makes you so sick all the time?" Aukina asked.

It was the moment I had been dreading. Did I tell them the truth about who I was and the decisions I had made that led to this place? Or did I hide away the flaws, leaving them clueless as they tried to help?

I studied the faces of the three women before me, all younger by centuries. Satella was the closest to my age, but the other two were babes in comparison. Yet, they all looked bright-eyed and hopeful. They cared, and they were willing to help me.

It didn't feel real. Having others who cared about my health, my life.

"When I use my magic, it drains my physical health." It wasn't the whole truth, but it was a start.

Satella lifted her eyebrows, but she kept her lips pressed in a tight line. She had been treating my ailments for five decades, and I had never admitted the truth behind them. Her face said more than enough. She was pissed I had never told her this. It could have changed her treatment.

Only, it was difficult to believe that. Even now, there was a kernel of doubt that the beings staring up at me could do anything. My health and power were tied to a demon in a bargain no one but the demon himself could break. But if there was any hope, it was in the hands of the friends in front of me.

"Reamann and I host a training class once a week," Aukina said. "It's meant for self-defense, but I'm sure he would be willing to help you train to strengthen your body. If you are physically stronger, maybe your magic wouldn't hurt you as much."

I typically avoided strenuous activities, since it had triggered breathing attacks in the past, but I was willing to give it a shot. I didn't want to die. I didn't want the magic that once saved me to be the thing that tore me apart, even if it had kept me alive well past my mortal life span.

"Do you really think it will help?" I wasn't sure how I felt about joining a class with others. The last thing I wanted was to look weak in front of anyone, but I tried to remind myself that if I didn't want to succumb to my sickness, I had to make an effort.

"It's worth a shot. The next class is tomorrow," Aukina said. "After lunch. Try not to eat a heavy meal."

Phase one of my friends' plan to help me was to physically strengthen my body. Phase two was to search for a magical cure which I already knew didn't exist. Phase three was up in the air, to be decided if phase one and two failed.

As I approached the barracks outside the estate, I pulled at my fingers. I had promised Aukina I would give it a shot, and I didn't want to break my promise, even as the urge to return to the confines of the library tugged at my chest.

The barracks smelled of sweat and dirt. There was an open space in the center that was marked off to define the training area. The wall behind it was lined with weapons ranging from bladed weapons to maces to bows.

To the left side of the room, heat surged and the sound of metal clinking against metal echoed out of the nearby room. The smell of molten iron pierced my nostrils, and my nose scrunched as my magic recoiled. Demons were weak against the metal, but the stronger the demon, the less effective the metal was. It was nothing compared to tenisium. The black metal repelled all magic, demon, fae or otherwise. It was a rare substance, though. Only bits and pieces were known throughout the five demon kingdoms.

"Tareen!" Reamann waved to me, but I didn't join him. He was talking to a fae male with blond hair. I wasn't familiar with the other guardsmen. I didn't leave the library often, so despite being one of the oldest residents, I didn't know many faces or names of the newcomers, especially if they didn't visit the library.

Reamann finished saying something to the blonde, before they both walked over to me. I had hoped the fae would leave to do something else, so I didn't have to interact with someone new on top of training with a bunch of strangers.

Luck was not kind to me.

"Tareen, this is Iolas. Iolas, this is Tareen, the librarian." Reamann wasn't wearing a shirt, revealing rows of toned muscles, making me think Aukina was lucky to get a male as attractive as him to fall for her.

Iolas bowed his head slightly, his soft hair swaying from the motion. He wore a shirt, but the cut sleeves revealed muscular arms and a body to match. "Reamann has told me a bit about you." My eyes widened as I looked back at the orange-haired demon, wondering what he had said about me. Before panic set in, the fae continued, "He said you wanted to work on getting stronger."

Nothing about my magic being the source of my problems, I hoped.

"My lungs are weak, so I haven't done much before." I studied the fae's face, waiting for it to sour with judgment. Too many times others had told me if I worked out, I wouldn't have been fat. It wasn't that simple, but no one seemed to understand that working out in my condition wasn't easy.

"Then we'll have to work around that." Iolas smiled with ease. It wasn't bogged down by pity or by judgment.

Reamann clapped the fae on the back. "Iolas has offered to help you out a few times a week if you want additional training. He used to train new warriors in his old kingdom, so I figured he is good with beginners."

Most of the fae resided in Valenmae, the demon kingdom by the sea. It was their land before the demons took over ruling, but since then, the fae had spread across the continent, since not all of them agreed with the demon rulers. I was sure Iolas had originated from there, but how he ended up in Kinzlea was a mystery.

"Where is everyone else?" I asked, unsure of what to say to the fae directly. "You said to meet after lunch, and it's after lunch."

"The class trickles in as they finish eating," Reamann said. "They'll be here soon, I'm sure."

My chest tightened, making it difficult to breathe. I didn't like showing up late, but others didn't hold the same sentiment. It was frustrating on a good day, but I didn't want to say anything. I was a guest. I didn't have the right to tell others when to show up.

Others began meandering into the barracks, ready for the training class. The more people that showed up, the more uncomfortable I became, hating that I barely knew anyone. I stood in the corner, trying to look as invisible as possible.

When Aukina walked through the entrance with Satella, my chest collapsed with relief. When they saw me, they headed straight for me.

"I'm so glad you actually came!" Aukina said.

"I said I would." I didn't like to go back on my word. It was one of the few things I had going for me.

"I'm just glad you were feeling well enough," Aukina clarified. "I'm going to say hi to Reamann, but I'll be back."

I turned my full attention to the vampire. "You didn't strike me as the type to join a self-defense class."

"I'm not. I don't need it, and I can't risk breaking my nails." Satella flashed her manicured hands. They were an ombre of purple and pink in honor of her girlfriend. It was the most color the vampire had in her outfit, other than her deep red eyeshadow that matched her eyes. "Think of me as emotional support tonight."

I looked down at my own hands. The nails were plain and cracked. Another weak point caused by the magic running through my veins. "I wish I could have nails like that."

"You should see Elcy. She does my nails for me. I'm sure she could do yours, too."

Elcy was the teacher at the estate. She came to the library with the children every once in a while to encourage them to read more. I hadn't realized she was the one who did Satella's nails.

"Maybe," I said. I didn't know how to approach her about that.

Reamann clapped his hands together, saving me from a response. "Let's get started."

Chapter
14

B y the time the training session was over, sweat poured down
my neck, and my lungs ached. I couldn't remember a time
when my entire body felt sore like that. After the others left, Reamann approached with a container of water and offered it to me.
He said nothing as I took long sips.

When I handed it back, he finally asked, "How was your first
session?"

"Hard." Breathing was easier than I had anticipated, but my
stomach twisted, a wave of nausea washing over me. Slow breaths
pushed back the need to vomit, but just barely.

"I'd say it gets easier, but that'd be a lie."

I looked at him with wide eyes. "If it doesn't get easier, then why
bother?"

Reamann took a long swig of water. He had a slight sheen to his
face, but he hadn't broken out in a full sweat like me. "Because
with each session, you are getting stronger. If you are working out
properly, you should push yourself harder. The work doesn't get
easier, but you get stronger, mentally and physically. In that way, I
suppose it can feel easier."

"I don't know if I can handle this." The thought of walking back on shaky legs made me nervous.

"I know you can." Reamann's smile didn't falter. For a demon, it was as if he was made of sunshine. He was different from all the other demons I had come across. Even King Zathrian had cruelty hidden behind his kind eyes.

"But it's so hard." I pressed my hand against my chest. I had nearly pushed myself over the edge, but thankfully, the class had ended before that.

"Anything worth having is worth fighting for." Reamann clasped me on the shoulder, his large hands steady.

As I made my way back to the library, I mulled over the orange-haired demon's words. It had been a long time since I fought for anything with substance. After being attached to a wooden pole and set on fire for making potions in the village I had once called home, I fought for the strength to fight back. I fought for the power that would make me superior to others.

Since then, I hadn't fought for anything other than peace.

I wasn't sure if that could have been classified as fighting. Hiding in a library was the opposite of fighting. It was hoping the world had simply forgotten about me. I wasn't worth fighting for. Not anymore.

I barely noticed Jathral's magic as I stepped into the walls of the room that had become my home and the closest thing to a friend I had since arriving at Ethlow. That was until Satella, Aukina, and Nyri decided I was worthy of their friend group.

The demon king was off in some corner, his magic twisting in the air as he searched for whatever it was he needed from my library. I moved straight to my room. After training my body for an hour straight, I didn't have the energy to deal with him.

I was nearly there when a wave of fury crashed through the room, and a crack echoed in my ears. My hand stopped midair as I reached for my door handle. My stomach twisted, knowing what that sound was. Rage bubbled up, combating the tiredness in my bones. My fingers twitched, debating if it was worth the argument.

My body said no, begging me to slip into my room and ignore the sound of destruction. My pride wouldn't let me. I had given the demon king one rule to follow, and I was sure he had broken it.

My feet moved, ignoring my muscles' protests. It didn't take much to find Jathral standing in front of a broken shelf with books scattered on the floor. My vision went white, and my veins burned, making my entire body shake.

"What did you do?" My voice was low, but rage seeped out with every word.

Jathral turned to me, his amethyst eyes flickering. His power poured out of him in waves of heat. "Where is it?"

"You broke the one rule I set for you." I ignored his question. He didn't deserve a response when he stood in front of a broken shelf. To him, it was just another piece of furniture that could be replaced, but I knew the truth. There was a life in the bookshelves, one I didn't fully understand.

"I don't care about your stupid rule," Jathral snapped. "Without that book, people are dying. *My* people."

"I don't care about your people. I care about my library." I knew how the statement sounded, but I wasn't about to back track—not when it came to Jathral.

"I'm not surprised a heartless witch doesn't care about my people. You wouldn't care if the world around you burned as long as you stayed hidden in the walls of this desolate place." Jathral sneered, flashing four canines sharp enough to tear out my throat.

My skin burned as magic thrummed through my muscles. It begged me to unleash it against the demon king. It wanted to tear him down and bring him to his knees more than I did, which was saying something. But if I used my powers to tear him apart, it would come at a cost, one I wasn't willing to pay to teach Jathral a lesson.

"I would rather stay in these walls than act like an ass to everyone I meet." I curled my fingers. Sweat coated my palms, and my heart thundered in my ear. The destruction at Jathral's feet was the reason I didn't want to let the demon into my library. I should never have let him in, no matter what Viridian had offered.

Jathral clicked his tongue. Heat pulsed off him, as if his magic was demanding to be unleashed, like my own. "You're ignorant, witch. For your age, I thought you would understand the world better. Instead, you hide from it while acting superior."

"Get out," I snapped. My palm burned in warning against the deal I had made with Viridian. I had given rules for Jathral to follow, but they weren't part of the deal made with the master of the house. Jathral could tear down every shelf and burn the books to oblivion, and there was nothing I could do to stop him from entering again. Going against Viridian's deal could burn my soul into oblivion.

Whether Jathral knew that, I didn't know. If he did, he'd become insufferable. He already was.

"No." Flames danced on black claws jutting from his fingers. His body shifted, his skin turned leathery and a shade of red. His wings stretched from his spine, and he grew taller. The sight would have sent a regular human running. Jathral turned himself into the depiction of evil that tales told about humans, but it could have been worse. That form wasn't the demonic form of the underworld. No. It was tame compared to that.

I stood taller, even though I couldn't shift my body like the demon king. There was nothing I could do to alter my appearance to look more intimidating. Using my magic wasn't an option, either, not when I was already worn out. The only thing I could do was face Jathral and not flinch.

"I'm not afraid of you." I should have been. Even if I used every ounce of my magic against Jathral, he could destroy me. His power filled the air in my lungs, expanding with that threat.

The demon king's eyes burned with everything he had, but I did not falter. I did not fear him. He blinked once. Twice. Something simmered beneath the surface, but it wasn't the kind of rage that would burn the library down. There was a flicker of fear, and...

Jathral strode towards me, roughly grabbing my arm. "You should be afraid, and you're a fool for not being so."

Flames engulfed us, the heat blasting every inch of my body as my eyes filled with fire. Only Jathral's amethyst eyes remained. Then it was cold. Icy wind blasted the sweat dripping down my neck. White reflected off the ground, making the sun nearly blinding. The smell of snow and pine mixed with ash.

We were no longer in Kinzlea.

It was too cold for that. Snow was weeks away from falling in the northernmost part of Kinzlea. There was only one place Jathral could have brought me that would reflect winter this time of year.

Mithcourt.

I turned to the demon king next to me. He had shifted back to the demon form I was used to. Simple spiked horns, tucked in black wings, and the rest more human than anything. He looked out from the cliff we stood upon, staring at the dark, billowing smoke, turning the sky gray, even without a hint of clouds.

"My kingdom is burning."

I barely heard him over the howling wind, but the words hit their mark.

I walked past him until the cliff revealed a valley below. The ground was black, and only the remnants of a town remained. Homes had been reduced to ashes, with the exception of the stone fireplaces designed to keep the former occupants warm. The main street that could have held a marketplace was in rubble, the stone path shattered. Then I saw them, the blackened lumps that could have been only one thing.

I swallowed hard, the smoke irritating my throat. I counted at least a dozen of them, some of them too small.

"What happened?" My voice sounded too damn loud in the wake of the destruction.

Jathral's heat hit my back, but his fire wasn't enough to thaw the icy arrow stuck in my heart. "The veil between Mithcourt and the underworld is wearing thin. My powers are not enough to protect my own people and keep it sealed."

"This was an attack from the underworld?" My throat burned, but I pushed back the waves of questions. The creatures of the underworld didn't belong in the mortal realm, but they slipped through cracks. It was only ever one or two at a time, according to the texts I had read. One or two should have been nothing for a demon like Jathral to handle. One or two couldn't have destroyed a town like that.

"It was a decimation in the middle of the night in a town that had never experienced creatures of such darkness. The dragon fae who heard the screams of their family flew away, but too many perished." Jathral didn't touch me, but his warmth was enough to melt the snow around us.

I stepped back, letting the icy wind chill the bile rising in my throat. "I don't understand how this happened. My research—"

"The world is more than your books, little mouse." Jathral turned his gaze away from the destruction below us, putting his full attention on me. "When you leave your little haven, you'll find that the world is still burning."

"Take me home," I whispered, unable to find the strength I had a few moments prior.

"Can't handle the real world?"

I gritted my teeth and met his eyes. I found my strength again. I wasn't going to back down. "Take. Me. Home."

Jathral huffed, and the world erupted into flames the moment he touched my arm. My legs shook, but I refused to sit or lean against anything.

"Now you understand this isn't a game for me. You have an ancient text in this library that can save my kingdom. Where is it?" He was confident that the book was in my library, but he hadn't given me a title or description.

"You destroyed my library and think I will give in to you just because you showed me the struggles of your kingdom?" I asked. Before he could respond, I pressed on. "If you cared about your people, you'd put your pride aside and apologize for your arrogant attitude. If you can't do that, then any suffering your people go through will be your own fault."

I turned to walk away, but Jathral grabbed my arm. "Are you that heartless?"

"Are you that prideful?"

Jathral's grip slackened, and I walked away.

Chapter
15

T he screams of children echoed throughout the library, making me flinch. It was the day the teacher of the estate planned
to bring the children to get books, but their volume always caught
me unprepared.

"Good morning, Tareen," Elcy chirped as she entered the library
holding the hand of Nieven, a dragon fae who couldn't control her
fire breathing yet.

"Good morning." I eyed Nieven, nervous about her entering the
library. I knew she'd never intentionally hurt the books, but she
was prone to accidents.

Elcy released Nieven's hand before bending forward to make eye
contact with the girl. The pixie didn't have to bend far to meet the
child's gaze, her short stature keeping her close to the ground.

"Remember the rules. If you feel your nose itching in the slightest, get away from the books." Elcy poked the child's nose with a
smile. "Now hurry along to pick out your books."

I bit my inner cheek, trying to stop myself from saying anything.
Nieven had been to the library several times, and she had never caused damage before. However, I had heard enough rumors

about the child causing fires throughout the estate. It made me nervous to let her run free through my library.

"She's been talking all week about this trip," Elcy said, settling into a nearby chair. Her white freckles sparkled in the light, but it didn't hide the dark circles under her eyes. "She loves stories about pirates."

"The fantasy version or the real version?" I slipped into the chair next to Elcy, ignoring the urge to follow the children around to make sure they didn't destroy anything.

"Both." Elcy's laugh was like sunshine on a spring day. She sparkled in the way pixies were described in literature, but there was more to her beneath that facade.

"Good. It's important for children to know the truth about the world. Fantasies are fun, but they can lead to dangerous notions." A world ruled by demons wasn't one that brought dreams to life.

"I like fantasies," Elcy said, her smile brightening the world. Pixie dust glimmered on the edge of her aura. It was a little disgusting at how happy she looked. I didn't know why she had come to Ethlow, but everyone's story was the same when boiled down to the facts. The life they wanted didn't work out, and they had nowhere else to go. The details didn't matter.

"Fantasies give us hope," she continued. "I think there needs to be more hope in the world."

"Hope doesn't fix anything." My words were blunt, making the pixie flinch.

"Not alone, but hope gives people something to fight for, a reason to make a change." Elcy stared at the windows across the floor, barely visible through the bookshelves. It was as if she was looking into a future life that was better than the one she was in.

"It can also leave people waiting for a hero to save them from themselves." I knew that feeling too well. I had spent years waiting for someone to show up and save me. I had learned the hard way that there was only one person who could change my life in the way I had been so desperate for.

Elcy pursed her lips, looking around the room. "Satella mentioned you want to get your nails done."

I took a shallow breath. Satella had mentioned it before, but I hadn't planned on approaching the pixie about it. "Maybe. I don't want to bother you."

Elcy's wings fluttered, and gold dust floated in the air. It tickled my nose, making a sneeze crawl to the surface. She touched my hand. "I would be happy to do your nails. Come to my room in three days. I don't have the children then, so I will have plenty of time to do a set. Start thinking about what you want now."

I opened my mouth to thank her, but the sneeze overpowered my senses. My entire body shook from the force. I looked at Elcy, horrified by the display, but the pixie only laughed.

"Sorry. My pixie dust does that sometimes." Her wings tucked into her back, and the gold dust that shimmered around her disappeared. "Sometimes I forget to tuck my wings." She pushed a stray piece of hair behind her ear, smiling shyly.

Elcy was the definition of beauty in every way that mattered. Her golden hair looked kissed by the sun god, and her green eyes were as bright as grass on a spring day. Even with the extra weight on her body, she had the curves of a goddess. She had been blessed in appearances.

I shrank in her presence, wishing I had been blessed in the same way.

A shriek had both Elcy and me on our feet in an instant. That was not a cry of joy. It was one of pure terror, and as thick power filled the air, I knew exactly what caused the scream from the child.

With a flick of my wrist, my magic pulled my broom into my grip. I jumped onto it without thinking. I took off, leaving Elcy behind. Despite her wings, she didn't fly after me. I followed the pulse of Jathral's magic, ready to tear him apart. I hadn't seen him since our escapade to Mithcourt. If he showed up to terrorize a child, I wouldn't hesitate to throw up wards to kick him out, Viridian's bargain be damned.

Jathral stood over Nieven, his looming presence making the young child shrink.

"Leave her alone," I growled. I was moving too fast, and I knew I couldn't control my landing. I swerved in time to miss Jathral, but I didn't miss the bookshelf next to him. Books fell on top of me as I crashed to the floor. I didn't bother to count the bruises that would show up later. They were a daily occurrence for me.

"This is none of your business, witch," Jathral growled.

"My library, my business. Now get out." My voice was as icy as Mithcourt. I was tired of dealing with Jathral. He was a manipulative asshole that tried to make me look like the bad guy when he was the one who couldn't muster a simple apology.

"No!" Nieven grabbed Jathral's hand and stood between us. Her actions were idiotic, but I wasn't surprised. Children didn't understand the world or the dangers that came in a handsome package like Jathral.

"What's going on?" Elcy placed her hand on her side, struggling to catch her breath. If she had flown here, she wouldn't have struggled as much.

"King Jathral told me I could live at Mithcourt if I wanted." Nieven squeezed his hand, making the demon's eyes flicker in response to the contact with the child. He didn't look angry, which was a surprise. He seemed like the type to hate children and purposely make them cry.

"What are you talking about?" Elcy's eyes were wide as she took in the horns on Jathral's head. As a magic user, she was able to sense the immense power coming off the demon king. Her pale face was proof of that. "Nieven is a resident of Ethlow. You can't take her."

Jathral turned his full attention to the pixie. "I do not wish to take her anywhere. I am not fit to raise a child, especially one so young and incapable of controlling her powers." He glanced at me as he said, "If it wasn't for me, this child here would have set your library on fire. You should thank me for saving your precious books."

I ground my teeth. I needed to stand up, but I struggled to get my feet under me. I felt like a turtle stuck upside down.

Jathral turned back to Elcy. "I simply offered the child a place to stay once she was old enough. Dragon fae don't belong in Kinzlea."

Most live in my kingdom, so I thought she might want to be with her people."

"My name is Nieven," the dragon fae piped.

Jathral blinked once, slowly looking at the girl. The corner of his mouth twisted into a crooked smile. "I was telling Nieven she has a place in Mithcourt if she ever desires it."

I was stunned by the generosity and the gentleness of the demon king's voice when he spoke to the child. I steadied myself on my feet, but my anger petered out. "What was that shriek?" I was grasping at straws, desperate to hold onto any kernel of hatred I could find. Jathral destroyed the library. Being kind to a child didn't change that.

"I ran into him by accident, and it scared me. I sneezed and nearly set everything on fire." Nieven hung her head in shame.

Elcy took Nieven's hand, gently pulling her away from Jathral. "It's okay. You'll get control over it with more practice."

I licked my lips, unsure of what to say. If Jathral hadn't been there to put out the fire, there could have been serious damage. The demon king's eyes slid over to me, as if he could read my thoughts. I refused to return his gaze.

"Magic takes lots of practice. That's how I got as skilled as I am," I said to the girl. I waved my hand, creating a small ball of light.

"That's incredible!" Nieven said. "I want to do that one day."

"Maybe if you work hard enough, you can, but it's hard to get this level of control." I smiled proudly, remembering all the hard work I had put into honing my magic abilities.

"I'm going to practice all the time!"

Elcy grabbed the girl's shoulders. "Not all the time. Only when you're not somewhere you can set the whole estate on fire." A child's scream echoed through the bookcases, but this one came from laughter. Elcy cringed regardless. "We should get going before any real damage is done."

I wasn't about to argue with that. I waited as Elcy headed towards the front of the library, wrangling children as she went. Dark power filled the air as Jathral waited in silence. I should've told him to get out of the library, but the anger that usually filled me when around the demon was nothing more than embers.

"Before you start yelling," Jathral said, breaking the silence first, "I fixed the shelf I broke."

I turned slowly, convinced I had misheard the demon king. I blinked twice, waiting for him to start laughing.

Jathral leaned against the wall, his muscles bulging at his biceps. His breath was steady, but his eyes whirled as he stared into my soul. "See for yourself if you don't believe me."

I followed the flick of his gaze to a shelf that looked nearly the same as the others but had a sheen to it that indicated its new age. I hadn't realized we were in the same part of the library. The shelves were always rearranging themselves. The floor was never in the same layout two days in a row.

I dragged my fingers over the newly polished shelves and the books that had been dusted. Immense care had gone into building the replacement piece of furniture. The wood hummed beneath my fingers. The library was satisfied with the replacement, so I had no arguments against it.

Jathral's heat hit my back as his breath brushed against my ear. "That's the closest thing to an apology that I'll ever give."

I flipped around and pressed my back into the shelf. It shouldn't have been enough. I wanted to break Jathral until he was begging for forgiveness on his knees, but as I looked up into his eyes, I couldn't bring myself to insult him.

Instead, I grabbed his tie, pulling his mouth to mine in a heated kiss.

Chapter 16

The sweet taste of honey on Jathral's lips drove me mad. I nipped his lip, holding his tie close to stop him from pulling away. His groan warmed my thighs, making me eager to get him between them. Jathral braced himself against the bookshelf behind me. The wood vibrated beneath me in warning. The library would not put up with this nefarious behavior, especially not against the brand-new shelf.

Jathral pulled back, sensing the same warning as me. His eyes burned with desperation, which made my knees weak. I didn't care if the passion between us was purely physical. He was an arrogant asshole that I would never commit to, and I was a solitary witch, content to be alone. That didn't stop the physical desire from welling inside of me. I was scratching an itch with the demon king. Nothing more.

I dragged him through the shelves, unsure of where to take him to escape the eyes of the library.

Jathral scooped me into his arms, holding me against his chest. His heart thundered, his lips swollen from our kiss. Flames erupted around us, quickly replaced by icy air. I barely caught a glimpse of the bed with dark red sheets before Jathral's mouth was on mine again. My back hit the soft mattress a moment later. He pressed himself between my legs, and the hardness that rolled into me made an animalistic grunt escape my mouth. It wasn't quite a moan. It was something deeper and more primal.

Jathral broke the kiss to look down at me. His chest heaved as his eyes caressed my face, but I didn't want him to look at me. I didn't want to think about the demon on top of me. I only wanted to feel the pleasure I knew he could give me.

I hooked my leg around his and flipped us over, using a smidge of my magic. I reached for the buttons on his shirt, but he brushed my hand away, ripping his shirt and the buttons with it. I stared down at the sculpted chest below me. The gods had nothing on the male beneath me, and for whatever reason, he wanted to use me for pleasure as much as I wanted to use him.

I grabbed his chin, forcing him to look at me. "I'm in control. Understand?"

Jathral interlaced his fingers behind his head. "Go right ahead, little mouse."

I wanted to smack that beautiful and infuriating smirk off his face. My fingers stung as they hit his cheek. I stilled, surprised by my actions. In any other situation, I wouldn't have hit the demon, afraid he'd turn on me, but it was different in the bedroom. "Say it."

Jathral glared at me, his eyes shifting from a violet to a deep burgundy. "You're in control."

I leaned forward, pressing the lightest kiss against his lips. "Good boy."

Jathral's powers surged at the praise, but he didn't move, other than resting his hands on my thighs. He stroked his thumbs in small circles close to my core. The gentle sensation made my breath hitch. Nothing about the demon king screamed gentle or obedient, but as he lay beneath me, that was exactly what he was.

When I was satisfied that Jathral would listen to my commands, I lifted myself up and wiggled out of my bottoms. Jathral's fingers were there in an instant, making the process move faster. Then his fingers slid between my thighs, stroking my core. He purred when he found me soaking already.

"A naughty little mouse, aren't we?"

"I'm not a mouse. I'm a queen, and I didn't say you could talk." I rolled my hips slightly, forcing Jathral's fingers to move to my entrance.

"If you're a queen, then you need a throne to sit on." He licked his lips, wetting them for me.

The corner of my lip tugged up. "Looks like I need to shut you up." I crawled up his body until I hovered over his face. I grabbed the headboard, the dark wood carved into two dragons facing one another. I lowered myself, careful to not put too much weight on his face.

Jathral grabbed my thighs, pulling them apart to give him the best access. "Don't hold back." My chest twisted. As much as I wanted to sit on Jathral and show him who was in charge, I hated the idea of putting my full weight on him.

"Tareen," Jathral said lowly. "If you want me to eat you out, then you need to sit on my face. Suffocate me with your body."

I lowered myself, and his tongue dove into me, stopping me from caring about the rest of my weight. The demon dug his fingers into my thighs, pulling me down harder, his tongue moving deeper. I rolled my hips, desperate for more friction. I didn't care if Jathral needed to breathe, not when his tongue sent waves of pleasure through my spine.

I moved faster, my thighs burning from the motion, but the tired muscles didn't matter. Not as the pressure in my core built to unbearable levels. I needed a release, and I was close.

Jathral moved in and out of me expertly, matching my rhythm perfectly. He moved his tongue back and forth from my entrance to my clit at a pace that didn't feel possible. But then he pushed deeper while flicking the sensitive bud, and I knew there was more than one tongue at work. Jathral didn't stop for a second. It was as if he didn't need to breathe as long as he was able to delight in the taste of me.

The orgasm that hit was the slow kind, starting at my toes and moving through my nervous system until every inch of my body burned with pleasure. Jathral lapped up my juices, even as my grip on the headboard slackened. Exhaustion replaced the pleasure, and my eyes grew heavy.

Jathral wrapped his arm around my waist and flipped me over, so I was beneath him. The sudden movement sent a surge of energy through my body. I stared up at Jathral's sharp features, his desire burning brighter than ever before.

He reached down, grabbing his waistband.

"What are you doing?" I licked my lips, my eyes moving between his thighs, wondering what was beneath his clothes.

Jathral paused what he was doing to lean in close to my face. "It's my turn." He nipped my lip, the pain deliciously sweet.

The rest of his clothes disappeared in a matter of seconds, exposing him completely. I stared down, and my mouth watered. His size was unlike any human I had been with. "It's so..." I couldn't find the right word.

Jathral smirked. "Like what you see?"

My cheeks flushed. I didn't want to answer his question. He didn't need the ego boost. "No." It was an utter lie.

He cocked his head to the side. "If it's not enough for you, I can change that." His power surged through the room before I could answer. Shadows shifted around his groin, revealing two dicks instead of one. "Or maybe you want more." Another surge of power resulted in four cocks, and my throat went dry.

"One is good," I croaked.

He cocked his brow. "Just good?"

I felt my control slipping, and I didn't like it. "Just fuck me with one dick already," I growled.

Jathral's smirk deepened. "If you're that desperate for me, I suppose I can comply." In a flash, he had only one cock, and he didn't waste time pressing it into my entrance.

"Asshole," I moaned, barely able to hang onto my irritation as he stretched me out.

"You like it," he muttered in my ear. He thrusted again, jumbling any of my thoughts at the pleasure coursing through me.

"Fuck you." My breath was shallow, and I never wanted him to stop.

His teeth grazed my neck, making my body squirm beneath him. "I'm the one fucking you now."

His arrogance and confidence were more than any one being should've had, but as he moved in and out of me, I couldn't find it in me to try to put him in his place.

"You don't need this anymore." Jathral grabbed my shirt, pulling it over my head.

I scrambled to stop him, but he was faster than me. My breath turned shallow and quick as I lay naked beneath the demon. I didn't like being completely naked in front of anyone, because it allowed them to see me. All of me, including the part of me that I had been desperate to hide.

Jathral's eyes darkened as he took in my breasts, but as he looked lower, his entire body stilled inside of me. I knew exactly what made him freeze like that. It wasn't the rolls on my stomach. The demon king knew the shape of my body well enough with clothes on. No. It was the mark that was burned into my skin below my breasts.

Maroon stained my skin in intricate lines that formed the shape of a melting eye. It glowed faintly in the dim light, making it nearly impossible for the demon king to look away.

"What the fuck is that?" Jathral asked, his voice low and lethal.

I forced my breath to calm. I owed nothing to Jathral. He was an asshole and a demon king. Just because we were fucking, it didn't mean we meant anything to each other. I stretched my neck high, meeting the burning gaze of the demon inside of me.

"It's a brand from the demon I made a bargain with for my magic." I refused to be ashamed of the choice I made, especially when it was the reason I had lived long past my mortal life.

Jathral pressed his lips into a tight line. He hadn't so much as blinked since he saw the mark. His chest heaved, anger building in his veins. "You've been marked by another demon, and you didn't fucking tell me?"

I curled my palm, hiding the mark of Viridian, the second demon I had made a deal with. "It's my life. I don't owe you an explanation for something that happened centuries ago."

"Damn it, Tareen." Jathral pulled out of me and rolled off the bed. I hadn't thought his lack of presence would make me feel so empty, especially when I hated the bastard.

I grabbed the blanket and pulled it over my chest, hiding the brand from a lifetime ago. "You don't get to judge me. Not when I'm sure hundreds of women hold your brand on their bodies." Demons' power grew from the deals they made with mortals. As a demon king, Jathral was considered to be one of the five strongest demons in the mortal realm. As such, he needed deals to sustain that power.

Jathral flexed and curled his fingers repeatedly. The dim light of the room perfectly outlined his ass, but I forced myself to look higher, tracing the lines of his muscular back and the black feathered wings that emerged from between his shoulder blades.

"Who?" Jathral looked out the window that stretched from floor to ceiling, revealing the plains of snow outside.

"That's none of your fucking business," I growled.

Ragged breaths made Jathral's ribs shake. I didn't understand why he was acting like that. He didn't like me as much as I didn't like him. The thing between us was purely physical. Nothing more.

"What are the terms of the deal?" His voice was barely a whisper, but I heard him perfectly in the quiet air.

I debated telling him to fuck off. He didn't have the right to demand any answers from me. But the demon's mark on my skin burned in warning or from accidental use of my magic. I wasn't sure which. But it compelled my lips to open.

"I exchanged my life source for magic. Any time I use magic, no matter how little, it leeches part of my soul to the demon who owns me." My voice was steady. There was a time when I would've cried admitting that, but centuries had erased the dread that came with making a deal with a demon.

Jathral muttered something under his breath in a language I didn't understand. "That deal is why you're so weak."

My muscles tensed. They were sore from the training I had been doing with Iolas and Reamann, but I didn't care. "I am *not* weak."

Jathral finally turned towards me, and his face was as icy as the snow outside. "You nearly died because your lungs started failing you. That's the definition of weak."

My fingers dug into the blanket, the word echoing in my head like a taunt. Insults from the villagers from my home rang in my ear, calling me weak and pathetic over and over again. My magic scraped against my skin from the inside, begging me to unleash it. My rage made me want to listen to that call, consequences be damned. The only thing that stopped me was the way Jathral looked at me. If I used my magic, and my lungs gave out, it'd only prove him right.

"If you're not going to fuck me, then take me home." I let hatred from centuries of pain seep into my voice.

"No." Jathral disappeared into a plume of fire.

Chapter 17

I t was easy to figure out that I was in the demon king of Mith-court's bedroom once I wasn't naked. The snow outside the window placed me in Mithcourt, and the room was filled with ancient and expensive artifacts that made the room worthy of a king. The skeleton statue in the corner was something someone as egocentric as Jathral would have. The skeleton was posed as if it was holding up a pillar, and it looked as if it was about to be crushed under the weight.

Part of me wanted to destroy Jathral's room. An hour had passed since he left me without an explanation. I stared at my hand, knowing I could call on the deal with Viridian to take me back to Ethlow, but that was a waste of the Shadow Slinger's powers. He was the next best thing to a demon king. The deal was better spent in other ways, such as destroying everything Jathral cared about to teach him a lesson.

The black symbol of a bat on my palm burned with desire. It wanted me to call in the deal. I curled my fingers, hiding the image. Not yet. Not for this.

I couldn't sit still any longer, so I tried the door. It was unlocked and swung open with ease. I glanced around, expecting a guard or someone to be blocking my way, but the marble hallway was empty. If I was a prisoner, Jathral wasn't smart about it.

My footsteps echoed as I took in the decorations lining the walls. Paintings were hung every several feet, most of them of Jathral. I rolled my eyes at the sight of the demon king in different outfits and positions. He even had one where he was mostly naked except a blanket covering his groin. He would. I moved faster, not wanting to give more energy to the asshole than was absolutely necessary.

At the end of the hallway, an obsidian staircase wound down several levels. I made the descent, and my thighs quickly protested. I had to take a break halfway through, the burning in my muscles too much. By the time I made it to the bottom, my lungs ached. I pressed my hand against my chest as I continued exploring. The entire estate was empty, giving it an eerie feeling. It was opposite to Ethlow. Zathrian's estate buzzed with life from the residents that filled the rooms. The library was one of the few places that usually held quiet in the walls.

The hair on the back of my neck pricked with each step I took. The energy of the estate was off, but I couldn't figure out what caused it. I searched through the various halls, unsure of what I was looking for. As I turned the corner, I saw two large ashwood doors with twisted black door handles. A breeze came from the doors, gently ruffling my hair. The invisible force called to me, pulling me forward.

The doors swung open with ease, revealing stacks of bookshelves that outshone the library I had carefully cultivated at Ethlow. There were twice as many levels with golden staircases placed around the room, swirling from floor to ceiling. Each piece of furniture was carefully carved out of darkwood. Mage lights floated high above, but they weren't necessary while the sun was out. The back wall was made out of glass that let in the light reflecting off the snow.

There wasn't a spec of dust in the immaculate room. It would take a team of workers to keep the tears of the earth from coating shelves. I ran my finger over the closest bookshelf, and an energy buzzed into my bones. It wasn't a team that kept the library in perfect condition—not with the empty estate the room lived in. Magic protected the books and the furniture. Powerful magic that could only belong to one being.

I swallowed, unsure of where to start. I had thought my library was the best in the mortal realm, but I was far from right. My library was a shack in comparison to the beauty before me.

I wandered the shelves until my feet hurt, picking up several books as I went. There was a nook with couches and blankets near the window. I curled up there with my pile of books and settled in. Maybe I should've been concerned about finding a way home. However, Mithcourt was too far away from Ethlow to walk, and my magic wouldn't last long enough to get me home.

Jathral wouldn't keep me prisoner—not when he needed my knowledge and my library. Although why he needed my library when he had this one made little sense. Getting back to Ethlow was a problem for later me to deal with. I had books to keep me company until then.

"I'm surprised to find you here."

I bolted upright, slamming my book shut. Hours had passed since I had arrived. The darkening sky was proof of that. My eyes were heavy after hours of cramming as much information into my brain as possible. Once I left this place, I would never come back. I never wanted to go anywhere with Jathral again after he left me alone all day.

In one of the most wonderful places in the mortal realm.

"What are you doing here?" My voice was gruff as I twisted to face the demon.

Viridian stood tall, a white gloved hand pressed against his abdomen. "I'd ask you the same thing, but I already know the answer." He looked me up and down. "I told you to make life difficult for Jathral, not to fuck him."

My cheeks burned as I glared at the master of Ethlow. "Don't worry. That's not going to happen again. That prick left me here, stuck with nothing to do."

Viridian's eyes slid over to the pile of books I was halfway through. "You seem comfortable enough."

I crossed my arms. "What did you want me to do? Sit around all day doing nothing, not knowing how to get home?"

"You could've called for me."

My palm burned, a consistent reminder of the debt I held onto. "I was just going to make that asshole take me home. I didn't need to call in my favor."

"I didn't say that." Viridian held out his hand. "You're a resident of Ethlow. It is my responsibility to protect you. It's almost dark, which means danger is coming."

I blinked at him slowly. At Ethlow, the veil between the underworld and the mortal realm thinned in the darkness of night. Demons' power originated from the underworld, and the more powerful a demon was, the more the creatures of the underworld desired their powers.

"I'm inside, which means I'm safe." Even if I was at Jathral's castle, I was safe within the warded walls.

"Not here. Let's not waste time. I don't want to fight anything to protect you." Viridian waited for me to take his hand.

I moved closer, but I hesitated. "Why isn't it safe here?"

Viridian clicked his tongue. "I don't have time to answer questions you should already know the answer to."

I gritted my teeth, ready to argue against Viridian, but a distant screech made my muscles loosen. I took the demon's hand, not interested in finding out what creature that sound came from. Shadows swarmed Viridian and me. The only light in the sea of darkness came from Viridian's glowing teal eyes. These were the shadows of the underworld, but they were tied to the master of the house. It was rare for a demon to master the shadows, which was how Viridian had come to be known as the Shadow Slinger.

When the shadows disappeared, my library materialized in front of me. My stomach twisted from the teleportation magic, and the master of the house kept his hand on mine, keeping me stable.

"Deep breaths," Viridian ordered.

"I'm fine." I fought against the nausea, desperate for it to pass.

Viridian huffed through his nose. "No wonder you are attracted to him. You're both stubborn as mules." His grip slipped from mine, forcing me to contend with the dizzy spell alone.

"I don't know what you're talking about." It was a lie, but I refused to pretend otherwise.

"You are both in denial, too."

"Denial of what?" My voice snapped like a whip. I was in no mood for cryptic conversations, not after the way Jathral left.

"Now that you are safely back at Ethlow, I have more important things to do than have this conversation." He took a single step, and shadows encased half his body.

I grabbed his arm before he could disappear. "At least tell me why there was nobody in that place?"

Viridian's shadows hovered as he scanned my eyes. "King Jathral lives alone to ensure no one suffers from the creatures that have been invading his kingdom. The veil has thinned in Mithcourt, and Jathral can't stop the underworld from invading, but you already know that." The demon pulled from my grip and disappeared into the shadows.

My chest sank. I preferred to be alone. It was easier that way, but I had the option to be with others. All I had to do was venture to the mess hall, and I was surrounded by chattering voices. I had friends to go to if I needed someone—as strange as that thought was.

But to be completely alone in a castle like that... I shook my head. That kind of loneliness would wear on me. No wonder Jathral didn't know how to play nice.

Jathral had shown me the destruction of that village, but he hadn't explained how it had happened or why he needed a book from my library. I had thought he had been trying to manipulate me, not realizing how desperate his situation had become.

I swallowed my own guilt.

I wasn't the one at fault. If Jathral had been honest with me... I wasn't sure I would've helped, my petty grudge running too deep in my veins to listen before.

Chapter 18

The door to Elcy's room had a sun carved into the corner. Many chose different designs on their doors to make their space feel unique to them. The sun was a fitting symbol of the pixie's personality.

My knuckles rapped against the wood three times. The door swung open, and Elcy smiled brightly. Her hair tumbled in blonde waves that nearly went down to the middle of her back. Whenever she was around the children, she had her hair in a bun on top of her head, so it was strange to see her looking free. Even her clothes were far from the nice dresses she wore when she stepped into her teacher's role. "I'm so glad you came!"

"I said I would."

Elcy shook her head. "You don't need to take everything so literally. Come on in." She led me to a station in the back corner of the room where she had supplies lined up. She got to work quickly, starting by soaking my hands and cleaning up my regular nails. She tested the flimsy nature of them, and I tried not to cringe. I hated the constant reminder of my body's weaknesses.

I wasn't weak. Not any longer. Not in the ways that mattered.

"You're quiet today," Elcy said. She made long brush strokes with her deft hands. She had done this hundreds of times, if not thousands. I didn't know the age of the pixie, but she had an old soul. There was no doubt about that.

"How can you tell if someone is a good person?" I hated Jathral. He was the worst kind of demon.

At least that was what I wanted to believe. After seeing his empty castle, it made me question it. He left me in the bedroom, mad about something that didn't matter. Then there was his claim about trying to protect his kingdom. I hadn't believed him, even when he showed me the destruction of his village. Did that make me the villain? Stopping him from getting something he needed to protect others.

"That's a complicated question." Elcy pursed her lips, her mind spinning for an answer. "In some ways, you can't know what someone is truly like. It's impossible to know what's going on inside another's head. You can pay attention to their actions, but that will only get you so far. You have to fill the gap with trust."

I scoffed. "How can you trust anyone in a world like this?" I had believed in the wrong person one too many times. It had turned my heart jagged over the centuries.

Elcy twisted the thin brush in a quick, swooping motion, creating a simple silver design against a black background. "I believe there is good in everyone, even those that seem to have the darkest hearts. They just need a little sunshine to clear the shadows."

I didn't know what to say to that. After living as long as I had, it made it difficult to believe there was good in everyone. Elcy was also an immortal, but she had stayed positive all of these years, even after life had been cruel enough to bring her to a place like Ethlow. I wanted to call her naive for believing in everyone, but she was doing me a favor by doing my nails.

"That sounds like a recipe for disaster. Someone is going to take advantage of you." The words sounded harsher than I had intended.

Elcy shrugged her shoulders. "Maybe they will, but I know those I open my heart to will be there for me if that happens."

Did I have that kind of support? My friendships with Satella, Aukina, and Nyri were new, but they acted like they cared. Aukina brought me food when I was sick. Satella worried about my health. Nyri had been nothing but kind to me. Their actions said they were trustworthy.

"What if someone does things that are both good and bad?" I wanted to believe Jathral was an asshole at his core. The things he had done were rude and inconsiderate, but even though he was a demon, I couldn't imagine him as evil. Not when he rebuilt the bookshelf and offered a home to a lost girl.

But then he left me in his bedroom without an explanation.

My head spun from the contradictories.

"Then I would follow your heart."

I tried not to gag at the pixie's advice. It was too sweet, and it was naive. The heart wanted things that weren't logical.

It wanted things like demon kings.

I scanned the bookshelves in hopes of finding the book on the elven perspective of the Great Demon War, but I barely paid attention to the titles that I passed by. For whatever reason, the library didn't want me to read about that particular history—something I didn't understand. It wasn't about something I had done to it to upset the being that lived in the walls. Every other book I had looked for, I found with ease.

Not that I cared today. Not when I couldn't get my mind off Jathral. I hadn't seen him since he left me naked on his bed with rage burning in his eyes. I didn't want to think about him and his lack of absence. I didn't want to care that he hadn't shown up after seeing the brand on my ribs, but his lack of presence meant one thing. He saw the demon mark and deemed I was unclean, just like everyone else who had seen it.

When I stopped walking, I found myself in front of one of the small windows in the library. It was nothing compared to the wall of glass at Jathral's castle. There were several windows in my library, giving a small peek into the world outside. Fall was nearly over. The trees were mostly barren except for a few leaves clinging to life. A storm was all it would take for the world to be ripped of the last of its color until next spring.

Heat pressed against my back, and for the briefest moment, I let myself lean into it. As the smell of snow and winter berries brushed against my nose, I was pulled from the lull of temptation.

I spun, and Jathral stood between two bookshelves, staring at me. Every muscle in my body tightened, remembering how he left me in his bed, alone and unsatisfied. I pushed back any sympathy I felt for him, knowing he lived alone to protect others. It didn't matter. Not when he treated me that way.

I waited for an apology I already knew wouldn't come. I deserved an excuse at the very least, but as the demon king's jaw feathered in frustration, I knew I wasn't going to get anything I deserved from him.

"No," I snarled. I moved before he could respond. I wasn't going to listen to him. He had his chance to grovel, and he wasted it.

Jathral followed at my heels. "Don't walk away from me."

"You *left* me alone, and you have the audacity to tell me not to walk away. That's rich." I ground my teeth together, forcing my body to move faster.

"I had a good reason for it." Jathral's snarl echoed through the hallway outside the library.

My thighs burned as I went from one hallway to the next. I didn't know where I was going other than away from Jathral. If he really wanted to stop me, he could have. Instead, he walked behind me with barely any effort to keep pace with my short legs. I stormed outside the estate, ignoring the stares after me.

"Stop." Jathral's voice was laced with exasperation, which only made me want to ignore him more.

"Leave me alone, Jathral." My feet crunched against the dead leaves that lay in a thick layer on the forest floor.

"No."

"You don't get to pick when you leave me alone and when you harass me." My lungs burned, and I knew I had to stop soon.

"Let me explain before you run off and hurt yourself." His presence overwhelmed me, and I felt him reach for me.

I lifted my hand and set a blast of magic towards the demon king. Jathral stumbled with wide eyes. He didn't believe I would turn on him. He had always thought I was weak, but I wasn't weak. I gave up everything, so I wouldn't feel pathetic.

My ribs tightened, my lungs taking the impact of the magic use. Air scratched against my throat as I attempted to calm my lungs.

Jathral gritted his teeth as he absorbed the blow. "Don't use your magic on me, Tareen."

He so rarely used my name, resorting to witch or little mouse most of the time. My name on his lips sent a shiver down my spine, but I shoved that feeling down.

More magic surged through me. "You don't get to tell me what to do."

"Don't be stubborn." Jathral stepped forward, ready to grab me. "You're hurting yourself."

"I don't care!" I screamed, letting the frustration of Jathral leaving me fill my voice. I was tired of being left alone. I was tired of feeling like I wasn't enough. I released the surge of magic spilling into my veins. A shimmering shield emerged from the ground, first blocking off Jathral from me before surrounding me in a bubble.

The blast of magic was more than I had used in a long time. My legs gave out, and I crashed to the ground. My palms scraped against a stick hidden beneath the leaves. The smell of blood filled my nose, but I didn't care, not as my chest squeezed my lungs.

The sound of Jathral's shouting was distant and muffled. I didn't understand what he was saying as his power whipped against my shield. His magic felt desperate, but the feeling faded as I struggled to take a proper breath.

Caw!

A crow sat on a branch, looking down at me. It cocked its head to the side, making light glint off the piece of jewelry in its mouth. It got caught in my shield and couldn't leave as long as it was inside.

Crows had been everywhere at the estate since spring. It was strange, since the smart birds rarely came near demons.

A pulse of concern flooded from the crow, and my eyes went wide. That wasn't a regular crow. Magic thrummed from the creature, chaotic with a touch of madness.

"What. Are. You?" I barely managed to ask with the shallow breaths plaguing my body.

Caw! The call sounded more like *Foolish witch.* If I hadn't felt the magic, I would've assumed I was hallucinating from lack of oxygen. *Drop your shield.*

The longer I kept my magic flowing out of me, the more it drained my lifeforce, but I felt stuck. It was as if the power had been waiting for me to lose control, so it could consume the last drop of my life. I had already used too much. "I can't." The realization made my hands shake. If I didn't turn off the valve that led to my magic, then I would die and prove everything Jathral thought about me right. My heart squeezed at the thought.

Not like this.

Caw!

The crow took off, but it couldn't go far with the shield. It flew above my head in tight circles before dropping a ring at my fingertips. A different magic pulsed from the piece of jewelry, urging me to reach for it. A green gem sat on top of a gold band. As my fingers brushed against it, a flash of green light blinded me. Warmth covered my skin, and then everything went black.

"Tareen!"

Chapter
19

Everything was warm, like being wrapped in a blanket in front of a fireplace in the middle of winter. I preferred the cold, but this warmth heated a part of me that had been crusted in ice. It was a dream. I was sure of it with how at peace I felt. I hadn't been at peace in a long, long time. It was difficult to do when I was contracted to a demon of sin.

I didn't want to open my eyes, afraid it would break the illusion, but with each breath, I didn't want to sit still. When I gained the courage to open my eyes, the flickering firelight against the shelves only confirmed the dream. I wasn't in my own library. There were no fireplaces there. I was at the library of Mithcourt.

I turned my head slowly, my body too heavy with exhaustion to move faster. Jathral stretched out on a couch, his chest rising and falling at a steady pace. As if he sensed my gaze on him, his eyes snapped open.

"Watching me sleep, are we, little mouse?" His lips tugged into a lazy smirk. A deliciously gorgeous smirk. I only allowed myself to think that way, knowing it was a dream. In a dream, I could pretend things were different.

"I was watching you drool."

His hand flew to his mouth, only to find a clean face. The chuckle that escaped my mouth sent my lungs into a coughing fit. Even in my dreams, my lungs were too weak to function properly. Jathral flew to his feet, dropping to his knees at my side. He took my hand with such gentle warmth. It made my heart flutter. In a different world, maybe I would've let myself fantasize about a life with the demon king, but I wasn't that kind of foolish girl.

Jathral would never want me in any way that wasn't physical, and I didn't want to be with a demon who couldn't apologize.

"Take it easy," Jathral said, squeezing my hand. Such gentleness that didn't belong to the demon king I had let between my legs.

"It's strange to see you like this."

He blinked, confusion softening his features. Dark circles painted his eyes, and the strain on his face wasn't from anger, like I was used to seeing. No, it was from genuine worry. I resisted the urge to laugh. I hadn't realized I was so desperate for affection that I would dream about Jathral being the one to give it to me.

"Like what?" the demon king asked.

"So caring." I knew better than to believe in fantasies.

Dreams were different. Dreams were just the mind's way of letting go and working out impossible situations.

Jathral blinked, unsure of how to respond to my comment. "I'm glad to see you're feeling well enough to mess with me." His voice was low in the way it was when he was irritated, but his eyes didn't hold the same weight. His irises held a lavender hue, another difference that didn't belong to the real world.

I settled on the couch, letting my fingers mindlessly stroke the blanket covering me. "I think I almost died." I remembered the moments leading up to unconsciousness. The fight with Jathral, the use of magic, the crow. It was strange being this conscious in a dream. I had never experienced it before. "Unless I did die."

Jathral hesitated. "You didn't die."

"How do you know?" I looked at my hands, wiggling my fingers. It didn't feel like I was alive. I felt too good for that.

"Because I wouldn't have let you die, little mouse. Who would I play games with?"

My heart fluttered, and I laughed. "Only if the real you would say such a thing. It's unfortunate this is a dream." I never would have admitted that to anyone, especially not the demon king. It felt good to feel wanted by him when he was between my legs. It made me crave the real thing. Someone who wanted me for me, bluntness and all.

Jathral rubbed his jaw, humming lowly. "A shame indeed." He stood, sliding onto the cushion next to me. He adjusted me, so I was cradled in his lap. His warmth filled my veins, making any aches disappear, even the ones in my heart. "At least there are no consequences in dreams."

"In some ways, maybe. In others, they make the heart yearn and ache for a reality that could never be." I nuzzled into the demon's chest, knowing it was dangerous to play this game, even in my own mind.

Jathral ran his fingers over my back, scratching it lightly. "Perhaps you're right." There was a resignation in his voice that kept me from falling asleep. If I closed my eyes, I knew this moment would disappear. When I awoke, I'd either find myself in the underworld or in the infirmary. I couldn't tell which one yet.

"Tell me, little mouse, why did you make a deal with a demon?" Jathral's voice was soft, as if he, too, were fighting off sleep.

"Because I wanted to watch the world burn the way they burned me. I wanted everyone to stop looking at me like I was just a pathetic human woman. Everyone always judged me for my looks, never stopping to realize my body didn't define who I was on the inside." That judgment had never stopped, even with great power at my fingertips.

"Did you burn them?"

"To ashes." There was no remorse in my voice, but I waited for the judgment to come.

"Good." No disapproval, but there was a hint of pride. "Tell me what demon you made the deal with?"

My body tensed at the question. I hadn't spoken the demon's name since I made the deal with him. If this wasn't a dream, I would've kept my mouth shut. The real Jathral didn't deserve the truth after the way he treated me.

This wasn't the real Jathral. He was too gentle, too caring.

"Aburon," I whispered. My brand burned with the demon's name on my tongue, but Jathral's hand was there a moment later, soothing the sting.

Jathral was quiet for a long moment, so long I thought he had fallen asleep. "Don't use your magic again. Aburon is dangerous, and he will kill you if you aren't careful."

The instinct to fight was gone in this dream world. "I know." I didn't want to die. There was more I wanted to do. I wanted to help Nyri cultivate the bleeding heart lilies and make healing potions, so others could be saved. I wanted to read about elven history. I wanted to fall in love—even if I denied it. When I saw others in love, it made me want to know what it was like.

"I will die eventually," I said. I feared my time would come sooner than later, especially if I couldn't control my emotions and magic around the real Jathral.

"Not if I can help it." His voice was soft.

I craned my neck to look at him, unsure if I heard him correctly.

He cupped my cheek and smiled unlike I had ever seen before. It was stunning and heart-wrenching. "Sleep, my little mouse. You need your rest." He pressed his lips against my forehead, and I stopped fighting the darkness.

My body ached with a heaviness that went deep into my bones. I cracked my eyes open, taking in the pinned bugs on the wall. I was in the infirmary, still alive, even if every part of me ached. My chest caved in, a second wave of loss washed over me.

It had been a dream after all. A small part of me had hoped it was real, and there was a side to Jathral that actually cared about me. Dreams led to dangerous hopes, and the weight of the real world was unbearable. It made me want to fall back to sleep, to let the warmth of the dream wash over me again, but that was the unfortunate thing about dreams. No matter how good or peaceful, I couldn't force them into existence.

A warmth pulsed around my middle finger. I brushed my thumb against a gold band, feeling the magic embedded in the simple piece of jewelry. My magic pressed against it. The small use of magic made a sharp pain stab my ribs, but I ignored it. At the most basic level, there was a protection spell cast on the ring, but there was more to it. There was a deeper and more complex spell beneath, one I didn't have the energy to break down.

Maybe once I was recovered, I could look into the ring more and learn about its origin. If I could find that crow—that wasn't actually a crow—I could question it, demanding to know why it gave me the ring.

Later.

That all could come later, when my lungs didn't ache.

A door opened, and Satella's footsteps grew louder with urgency. She hovered above me, her chest heaving up and down. Anger laced her eyes. Proof that I had survived my own magic.

"You used your magic again." There was no question in the vampire's voice. "And you nearly killed yourself doing it."

I swallowed, but my throat was dry. I kept my breath slow and easy, afraid that too much air would trigger a coughing fit. "How long have I been out?"

Satella handed me a cup filled with an elixir. "Two days. I was worried you wouldn't wake up. Astoria assured me your soul wasn't ready." She sank into the closest chair. She didn't have to explain that the grim reaper's reassurance hadn't helped. The strain in her face said more than enough.

"I don't want to die." That fact had become more clear to me. There was a time when that hadn't been true. When the scars on my thighs pulled me to dark depths and twisted thoughts.

"You can't use your magic if this is what it does to you. I don't care what that fuckhole did to you. Your life isn't worth him."

I bolted upright, knowing she was talking about Jathral. My body whined at the sudden movement, but with the dream of him fresh in my mind, the mention of the demon king made my heart thunder.

"Where is Jathral?"

Satella's face soured at my question. "Who gives a shit? After he brought you here, I told him to stay away."

My heart thundered. That was the second time Jathral had saved my life by getting me to Satella. I hated feeling like I owed him. At the same time, my heart squeezed.

"He hasn't visited?" The dream felt more like a memory. It was almost as if I could smell the winter berries on my skin after falling asleep in his arms.

"No. He was an asshole about it, saying I couldn't tell him what to do. I told him where he could shove it. He stormed off and never came back." Satella shrugged. "At least he is learning not to argue with me."

A few weeks ago, I would've delighted in Satella's story. Instead, the muscles around my heart constricted, making it ache. It was a foolish emotion. I knew better than to hope for Jathral to do anything nice for me. The dream was a version of the demon that would never exist. I tugged at my fingers, knowing that as the memory of the demon king faded, so would my ridiculous emotions about it.

Chapter
20

Nyri's fingers were covered in dirt after hours of digging through soil. Growing bleeding heart lilies was so much more than using her magic to make them grow and bloom. She encouraged blue bees to pollinate the flowers, helped the seeds grow, created new flower beds for them, planted the seeds, watered them. It was a process, one I didn't know how to help with, especially since I was on a magic ban, even from the simplest magic. It left me to do the most basic tasks that anyone could have handled.

I spread the dirt in the newest line of planters, ensuring the level was perfectly even and matched the others.

"That'll do." Nyri wiped the sweat from her brow with the back of her hand, accidentally leaving a trail of dirt behind. Despite the chilly fall weather, the glass walls and the magic of Zathrian kept the temperature warm and humid, perfect to maintain the plants that normally didn't grow in this season.

"You're not planting more seeds today?" I asked. In our attempt to recreate the purple flower variant, we ran out of bleeding heart lilies to experiment on. Nothing worked. Nyri tried kissing Zathrian while the flowers bloomed. She had brought Aukina and Reamann to display their affection. Every couple that was supposedly in love did little to stir the magic of the bleeding heart lily, leaving us at a loss.

Nyri looked at the sky. It was well past noon, and the rumble in my stomach said it was close to dinner. "We won't have time to work on it after eating, since it's been getting dark early. It's okay. One day won't hurt." She wasn't worried in the slightest, as if she had all the time in the world. Her human lifespan said otherwise, but I kept that thought to myself.

"Can I take some of these flowers?" I gestured to the bleeding heart lilies in full bloom. "I can use them to make potions and salves. It won't be as effective as the one I made for you, but it should help Satella out."

"Take what you need from this section." Nyri gestured to the oldest group of flowers.

I gathered a few, careful not to take too many. I only wanted to use what was necessary, especially knowing the price of the individual flowers. One sold to the right person could yield enough coin to feed a family for an entire year. The flowers were considered precious in the demon lands, but Nyri was changing that.

"I'm going to take these back to my room, and then I'll meet you and the others." I had found myself in a routine ever since I had healed enough after my last breathing attack. Jathral hadn't shown up since, either heeding Satella's warning or not caring enough to check on me. My chest tightened, but I ignored the sensation.

I enjoyed my routine. I spent a few hours in the library in the morning. After lunch, I joined Nyri in the greenhouse and helped her. It helped subdue the temptation to use magic to entertain myself, especially in the longer hours I used to spend by myself. Then we had dinner, and I went on my way to work on potions, sometimes with Satella, sometimes alone if I wasn't in the mood for company or if Satella's girlfriend happened to be visiting.

A week had passed like that without Jathral's presence bothering me. It was nice not arguing with the demon king.

As long as I kept myself plenty distracted.

I hurried to the library, not wanting to lag behind for dinner. It was different to feel like I was part of something. It was new for me, and I didn't want to mess it up.

"Tareen!" Elcy called out, walking my way.

"Oh, hey." I hadn't seen the pixie in the past two weeks, but she was beaming as brightly as usual.

"How are your nails holding up?" Her eyes went to my hands, covered in dirt from gardening with Nyri.

I wanted to hide my fingers, since they were dirty, but I didn't want to be rude. "They are holding up nicely, despite how they look." Gardening with Nyri wouldn't have been possible before. My nails would've cracked under the pressure of digging in the dirt.

"Good! Come back to me as soon as you need them updated." Elcy glowed in ethereal light. I had never seen a being light up the way she did, even other pixies.

"I will," I said, and I meant it.

"Oh, Vesper and I are going to the—" She cut herself off, looking around to make sure we were alone. With a lowered voice, she continued, "The secret tavern. If you want to join us, maybe it'd be fun."

I blinked once. If she thought that tavern was much of a secret, she was as naive as she was positive. A second blink as I processed her invitation. No one invited me to places. At least that had been my life a year ago. I didn't understand what had changed.

"I've never been to the tavern," I said to buy myself a few extra seconds of thinking.

"It's fun. We go weekly, so even if you can't join us tonight, maybe next week."

"Why are you inviting me?" I knew the question wasn't the type people normally asked out loud, but I couldn't figure out the answer on my own. It didn't make sense.

"Because I think you'd have fun," Elcy giggled. "Plus, you and Vesper have a lot in common."

I searched my memory for a Vesper, but I came up blank. I debated about not asking, but I knew it'd drive me crazy if I didn't know. "Who is Vesper?"

"Vesper, the chimera that goes to the library like every other day." When recognition didn't fill my face, Elcy continued. "They have moth wings."

"Oh! They are at the library all the time." I had seen the chimera searching the bookshelves for something new to read constantly, but they had never approached me. I didn't approach in return, respecting that they might have wanted to be left alone. They rarely stayed at the library for more than a few moments.

Elcy let out a long sigh. "Yes, they are. You should join us. I promise it'll be fun."

The thought of being in a tavern surrounded by new people made my heart race, but I didn't want to outright reject the offer. "I can't tonight, but maybe next time."

"I hope so! Vesper's waiting for me, but I'll see you soon." The pixie waved at me before practically skipping down the hallway.

I watched her, confused by the interaction. It was as if there was a shift in the universe, one where people actually *liked* me. I didn't know what to think of it, so I put it in the back of my mind, afraid I'd curse the blessings.

"Again," I wheezed. I pressed my hand into my side, fighting the sharp pain lacing my ribs. My stomach churned, and all signs told me to stop.

Iolas' face said the same thing. "I think we should finish for today."

"Again." Another week had passed without Jathral's presence.

Iolas dropped the wooden sword in his hand. "You can barely breathe, and if I push you too hard, Satella will kill me." The fae's cheeks tinged pink. He had a crush on the vampire—which wasn't surprising. She fed off him, and she was gorgeous. She'd easily steal the heart of any man or woman. If she hadn't been dating the grim reaper, I might have even taken a shot at her. It was a shame she was already in love.

"Satella won't kill bugs. She won't hurt you. Again." There was no need to push myself this hard, but after two weeks of not using my magic, my skin vibrated, as if it was desperate for a release.

I let my arm drop, the muscles screaming at me. I wasn't any good at sword play. Iolas humored me as I swung the fake sword around like a wild woman. It'd take years to master swordplay, and I didn't have any interest in fighting. The motion and exercise calmed my nerves and my mind.

"I need to go again." The less I moved, the more I wondered about why *he* hadn't come around in the past few weeks. I doubted Satella was enough to scare him away—not with that arrogance of his. But me...

If he had decided I was too much to handle, as so many did, I...

"Again." My voice cracked, and tears welled in my eyes. I tried to suppress the emotion but after weeks of avoiding my feelings, I couldn't do it anymore. I was too tired to keep fighting, and not using my magic made it worse. It was as if a steady drum had been beating against my skull, slowly getting worse with each day I didn't use magic.

"Are you hurt?" Iolas asked. His mouth twisted as he took in the tears sliding down my face.

"No. I'm fine. Let's go again." I lifted the wooden sword, my shoulder aching. I had already pushed myself too far, but I didn't care.

Iolas didn't move. "A good warrior knows when to rest. I won't fight you, but I'm here if you need to talk about anything."

I grunted, swinging the sword at Iolas. He thought I was too weak. Iolas lifted his sword to block my attack at a speed I barely registered. He grabbed the wooden blade of my weapon and twisted it out of my hands. He pointed both fake weapons at me, his jaw tight as he looked me over.

"We're done for today. Let me put these away, and I'll walk you back to the estate." Ever the gentleman Iolas was, but I didn't want that.

I walked away while the fae's back was turned away. The cool breeze hit the back of my neck, chilling the sweat covering my body. I relished the frigid air. It gave me something to think about other than a demon with magic flames. I would've stayed outside longer if I wasn't worried about Iolas catching up to me or the darkness threatening to bloom in the sky. It was an hour away from sunset, but that was enough time to get lost in thought or lost in the woods.

By the time I made it back to the library, my lungs ached, but it was different than the strain put on them by magic. It was the kind of pain that ripped the body apart to make room for more. I wanted more. I wanted to be stronger, so demons like Jathral didn't think of me as less.

I slid into the library and instantly froze. The smell of snow and winter berries was overwhelming. My heart raced as images from my dream flashed through my mind. I had hoped the dream would fade, but it had merely haunted me in my waking hours. Anger began to battle with the desire of foolish dreams.

Jathral stepped out of the shadows, his appearance ragged. His shirt had several buttons undone, and his hair was a mess around his horns. A sheen of sweat and dirt covered him, but there were no signs of his wings.

I didn't know if I wanted to yell at him or jump his bones.

Chapter
21

T he air was thick as our eyes locked onto each other. Jathral looked as if he was fighting his emotions as intensely as I was fighting mine.

"You look like hell," I said, defaulting to my insults, even as my heart fought to get free of my chest.

"Good to see you, too, little mouse." His eyes swirled as he stared at me. He didn't move closer, as if he was waiting for me to make the first move.

Thoughts of his arms around me made it impossible to keep his gaze. I tore my eyes away, heat finding my cheeks. Stupid dream. I could barely remember how to be mean to the asshole demon.

"You've been gone awhile." I picked up a book, pretending to not care about his response. I wondered if he could hear the ache in my throat with his pointed ears.

"Did you miss me?"

Was that hope in his voice? No. I was projecting.

"No." I pulled a pile of books into my arms and walked to the shelves to put them away. It was unnecessary, but it gave me a distraction.

"Liar." Jathral's scent followed closely.

The accusation made my anger flare, but I kept my mouth shut. I didn't have an excuse he'd believe. "Where have you been anyway? I thought you had important book business here."

Jathral plucked a book out of my arms. He hovered inches away from me as he skimmed the title. I hated the bastard. I had to tell myself that to stop my fingers from reaching for the stubble on his jaw.

"*The Whereabouts of Misfits and their Missed Fortunes?*" He cocked an eyebrow in question.

"It's not mine. Someone borrowed it and didn't put it back." I tried to grab the book, but the demon lifted it out of reach. "Are you going to ignore my question?"

"You must've missed me if you care so much." His lip curled in that infuriatingly delicious way.

"Nevermind." I set the rest of the books on the shelf, trusting the library to sort it in the way it was known for. I needed space from Jathral. I didn't know how to talk to him without my imagination running wild from the dream. I needed to remind myself that the Jathral following me through the library was a different demon.

One that was skilled with his tongue.

One that left me naked and unsatisfied in his bed.

"Something came up that was more important," Jathral answered, refusing to give me space.

"What kept you away for two weeks?" *Did you not care that I nearly died?* I kept the second thought private. I didn't want to know the answer.

"I checked on you." Jathral's voice was steady, even as I walked away.

My feet ached worse than my muscles, and all I wanted to do was sit down, but that would leave me trapped. "Satella said you didn't come by."

"What the vampire doesn't know won't hurt her."

Once again, my mind went to the dream, but I pushed that thought back. In the dream, I had been in a library—Jathral's library. Satella would've known if I had been whisked away while I was under her care. Despite that, I knew Jathral wasn't lying. There was no reason for him to lie about that—not when we could barely stand each other.

The pixie's advice came to mind.

It's impossible to know what's going on inside another's head. You can pay attention to their actions, but that will only get you so far. You have to fill the gap with trust.

In that moment, I made a decision.

I stopped in between shelves and turned to face the demon king. "What's the title of the book you've been looking for?"

Jathral hesitated. "*The History of Elven Magic: Volume 1: First Edition.*"

I knew that title. It was an ancient text filled with magic spells, many too dangerous for any mere mortal to cast. "That's part of my private collection." I shouldn't have told Jathral that. I had no real reason to trust him.

"Show me." It wasn't a request. It was a demand.

"I don't have to show you anything. My deal with Viridian only encompassed the main library. My personal collection is off limits to the regular residents." I didn't like anyone demanding I do something for them. It made me want to tell Jathral to leave, but a tug in my chest stopped me.

"Tareen—"

I put my hand up, stopping him mid-sentence. The control from that simple movement sent a jolt through my spine. "But as a thank you for saving my life twice, I will grant you entry as long as you promise to follow the rules."

Jathral's eyes danced. He was finally going to get what he wanted, which meant he'd be able to leave as soon as he finished his business with the book. It was best that way. My thoughts had become too twisted, and my anger wasn't enough to stave off the hunger for the demon in front of me.

"I can follow a few rules," he said with a slow smirk.

"Then follow me." My heart thundered. There were very few people I showed my private collection to. I had let Satella in there a few times, and Zathrian saw it once. I didn't trust anyone else at Ethlow with that kind of access. Jathral should've been the last person I trusted, but I was trying to listen to Elcy's advice. Between Jathral's recent actions and what my heart was saying, the demon king had good intentions.

I weaved in and out of bookshelves, and the library cleared the path to the secret room, as if it approved of my decision to let Jathral peruse my collection. As I reached the wall that held my secret chamber, I paused to look at the demon king. Before I let him in, I needed to hear that he would follow the rules.

"The most important rule is that you cannot take anything in that room out. Everything in there is ancient and precious." And dangerous, but I didn't want to give him any ideas. "If you damage anything in that room, I will kill you."

Jathral leaned in, his scent swarming me. "I'd like to see you try, witch."

The challenge made heat burn in my core. I wanted to show Jathral exactly how strong I was, but that would require using magic—something Satella forbade me to do until she was sure my body could handle it.

"The second rule is that you are not to venture in or out of the room without me as a guide. There are wards in there that can kill someone. In fact, the last person who didn't listen to me got herself into some trouble."

"You're worried about me." There was no question in his tone, which made me bristle at the implication.

"I'm worried you're too stupid to follow my instructions," I growled. I hated what that cocky tone did to my body.

Jathral wasn't phascd by my insult. "I understand your rules, and I promise to follow them."

I searched his face for any signs of a lie, but I couldn't find one. There were too many reasons not to trust him, but he saved my life. Twice. He had never hurt me, and he was trying to save his kingdom from being destroyed. Even if he was an asshole, it had become clear that he was an asshole who cared.

"Okay," I said, accepting his words. I turned away and pressed my hand against the wall. Magic that was no longer my own made the wall shift until it revealed a plain black door. "Create a light."

"Giving me orders now?"

I glanced over my shoulder. "I could create the light, but Satella put me on a magic ban since the incident."

Understanding flashed into Jathral's eyes. With a gentle flick of his wrist, a green ball of light appeared above my head. Satisfied, I reached between my breasts and pulled out a golden key with the head of a crow at the end.

I reached towards the door, but I hesitated. "Tell me why you left me alone in bed." My heart raced in anticipation of the answer. It was a stupid question to ask, and the answer shouldn't have mattered, but it did.

Silence filled the air, and for a moment, I thought Jathral was going to ignore me.

"I left to hunt the demon who has you under his claws."

My throat tightened. His answer didn't change anything.

Only it did.

I quickly unlocked the door, unable to respond. I didn't trust my voice to hide the confusion twisting around my heart. The door clicked open, releasing the first set of magic wards. A long hallway filled with darkness stood before us.

The prickle of magic caressed my skin in warning. At one point, the power fueling the nightmare hallway had belonged to me, but after I gave it to the hallway meant to keep out unwanted visitors, it twisted into something that I barely recognized.

"Keep that light on," I muttered. Despite the familiarity of the room, I knew how dangerous it could become if left unprotected. I didn't like relying on Jathral to keep our path illuminated, but I was trying to trust him. Trust was terrifying, and I didn't like it.

I walked with confidence through the winding path, and Jathral didn't falter behind me once. His magic likely sensed the dangers in the hallway just as mine did. Neither of us spoke until we reached the door that revealed my private collection.

Jathral shut the door behind him, but he kept the light going strong, even as the ceiling was illuminated by several balls of light. "You created that protection spell?" His brows lifted as he waited for an answer.

I shrugged. "I don't like people going into my space without permission." I went to the bookshelf at the very back and scanned the titles until I found the one Jathral was looking for. The tome was heavy. The cover had been created from a slab of obsidian with the title carved into it with silver paint to emphasize the markings. It was beautiful, as was every text created by the elves. They took care of their histories and knowledge, which was why reading about them was one of my favorite past times—if the library cooperated with me.

Jathral studied the shelves covered with ancient artifacts. Some of them I happened across during my time before Ethlow. Others I hunted until I found what I had been looking for.

"This is an impressive collection." Jathral locked his hands behind his back, not daring to touch the artifacts. "Not many can get their hands on this kind of power. I see why you don't let others in here."

Warmth bloomed in my chest. "I like collecting magic-imbued items, and I know they are better off with me than on the streets where someone without proper knowledge gets hurt or someone with proper knowledge uses it to cause harm." It was a point of pride.

"You could destroy kingdoms with this kind of power." Jathral's comment was casual, but it made my stomach twist.

"I'm not interested in destroying anything." I had done enough destruction for several lifetimes.

"Not even me?" Jathral moved to another shelf, inspecting it instead of watching for my reaction.

In some ways, I did want to destroy the demon king. I wanted to destroy his pride and make him beg on his knees in front of me. After spending more time with Jathral, it was clear he wouldn't bend for anyone, especially not a broken witch like me.

"I like the idea of you begging me." My eyes widened as I realized I had said the words out loud.

Jathral's body went tight. He turned slowly, looking me up and down. "Begging for what?"

After Jathral left me in his bed, I swore I would never let him between my legs again, but after that dream, it was hard to remember that. I wanted to feel him inside of me. I wanted to hear him moan my name as he spilled every last drop of his pleasure into me.

I set the book on the table, ignoring his question. "Here's your book. Call for me when you're done, and I'll come get you. Don't try to leave on your own. The hallway might attack, even with a light, since it doesn't recognize you.

"Or you could stay." His casual tone wrapped around my feet.

I pulled my fingers, knowing this was a bad idea. Staying in a room with little space with a demon I hated but wanted to fuck was a dangerous line to walk. "I didn't think you'd want my company."

"I just figured you would prefer to watch over me, since you don't trust me." His body was perfectly still as his eyes burned into me.

It should have been easy to tell him that I did trust him, but the thought got stuck in my throat. Trusting Jathral—trusting a demon—was a strange feeling, one I wasn't ready to admit to yet.

"Right," I breathed. "I had better keep a close eye on you."

Chapter
22

I flipped through a tome about simple magic those without powers could perform. *A Human's Guide to Tricking Immortals*. It was a ridiculous text, filled with thievery tools more than real magic. It didn't belong among the books about great magic spells or artifacts that hosted powers most dreamed of having. But it was a special book.

Jathral flipped through the book he had been desperate for, carefully touching each page. He took the proper care to handle ancient and fragile paper, something regular beings wouldn't understand. Between that, and the size of his library, he had an appreciation for learning that I wouldn't have expected from him.

"You're staring, little mouse," Jathral said, not taking his eyes off the text.

I looked back at my book, but I already knew every word on the page. I had read the book countless times throughout my life. It didn't take long for my eyes to return to the demon's face.

Jathral looked up to meet my gaze. "If you have a question, just ask it."

My cheeks flushed, and my instincts told me to insult the demon. "I didn't take you as the scholarly type." Not the insult I had wanted.

"That's not a question."

I cleared my throat, searching for the source of my inquiry. "You have the most impressive collection of books I have ever seen, and you are gentle with ancient texts. Many with power like yours don't appreciate scholarly activities, but you do."

"I still don't hear a question." He looked back at the book, flipping to the next page.

"Why?"

"Why do you care about knowledge?" he asked in return.

I traced the worn out words from the book in front of me. It was the first book I had ever owned, and I used it before I had bargained for my own magic. "Because knowledge is power. I'm too weak physically to protect myself, and my magic has limitations—as you have witnessed. But there are no limits to my knowledge, other than my own determination. The more I know about the world, the more I can control, and the more I can protect myself."

Jathral looked up from the book again. I felt his eyes on me, but I didn't look back, afraid I wouldn't be able to control my heart rate. With his demonic ears, I was sure he could hear every little change in the rhythm of my heart.

"A wise demon once told me that being strong and powerful is not enough to rule a kingdom. A good king studies his kingdom and the world to anticipate the needs of his people. Knowledge is power, just as you said. Having one kind of strength is not enough when you have a world on your shoulders." Such a thoughtful answer from a king that had a sharp tongue.

"I didn't think a demon would care that much about his people." It was true. I knew the five demon rulers were meant to protect their kingdoms, but that didn't stop the thieves or the killers. It didn't stop the starvation, either.

"I'm assuming you've read about the Great Demon War." I nodded, and he continued. "I'm sure you read about the destruction that came to the mortal realm when demons broke through the veil. Mortals and immortals of different races fought against the underworld to protect their lands. Countless died in that attempt, but it slowly became futile. Without closing the veil between worlds, the mortal realm was doomed. Do you know how the veil was closed?"

Out of all the histories I had read, few mentioned the breach in the veil. Most talked about fighting demons and even infighting from kingdoms that decided war was the perfect time to take over their enemies' territories. Many talked about resisting the demon conquerors that took over the lands.

When I didn't respond, Jathral continued. "The elves created a spell that repaired the fabric that separated the worlds, but they didn't have the power to enact the spell. Thankfully, there were five selfless demons who hated the underworld so much that they agreed to lend the power needed to close the veil."

I had never read about that part of the history before, and there were few old enough to remember the war. But Jathral had been there.

"Let me guess. They agreed to help in exchange for rule over the mortal realm?"

Jathral inspected his black claws. "A small price to pay in exchange for saving the world, don't you think?"

I wasn't sure if I'd called that a small price to pay, but saving the world was a large task. "And after you took the reins, you nobly started caring for your people?"

"Not exactly." Jathral closed the tome, capturing my full attention. "The five of us tried to close the veil, but even with our powers combined, it wasn't enough. We needed a sixth demon to step in and save us, to stop us from being destroyed by the underworld. It was our only choice, so we were forced to make a deal with him. He saved us, but in exchange, he said we had to rule and care for our kingdoms as well as wear his brand. He could've taken everything from us, became the emperor of the mortal realms, but he didn't. He didn't take advantage of us, like any demon would have, like I would have before all of that."

The itch to write down Jathral's account of the history made my fingers burn, but I didn't want him to stop. "So you walked away a changed demon?"

He leaned back, running his fingers through the side of his hair. "Something like that." His face darkened as a faraway look made his eyes glassy. "I swore to myself I wouldn't make deals with mortals that were harmful. You might think hundreds of women hold the brand of my bargain, but very few do."

"But demons sustain their power through their bargains." I didn't understand what the demon king was saying. He was considered to be one of the five most powerful demons in the mortal realm. He had to have made thousands of deals since he took rule.

"Exactly."

My chest tightened, absorbing the words of his story. It all made sense. The reason Jathral needed a book to protect his kingdom. The empty castle he lived in. Staying away from others to protect them, since he didn't have the massive power to protect them himself.

"That's stupid," I said. "If all you had to do to protect your kingdom is make deals with mortals, then why do you avoid it?"

Jathral's mouth fell agape. "You want me to take advantage of others?"

"To protect your kingdom, to rule as a proper king, why not?" Being noble was stupid if it meant being weak.

Jathral scoffed. "If you're so keen on me making deals, then why don't you make a deal with me?"

My heart thundered at the offer. "You have nothing I want." That was far from true, but the last thing I wanted was to be tied to Jathral for the rest of whatever life I had left.

"Not even access to my library? You seemed to enjoy it well enough." His voice turned honeyed, filled with sweet temptation that demons often used to lure in their prey.

"You mean after you abandoned me in your bed unsatisfied?" I raised my brows in challenge.

Jathral waved me off. "I sent Viridian to collect you."

Viridian hadn't said that, but I didn't want to let the new information throw me off. "Hours later."

"Hours after you got to enjoy my library. I know you were reading there. Your library isn't the only one that whispers. You were enjoying yourself." Jathral clenched his fists. He wasn't going to back down, and neither was I.

"It was okay, I suppose. I was simply making the best out of an awful betrayal." That was the understatement of my life. His library was a dream in so many ways.

"You don't have to pretend you didn't have a good time, and I already told you why I left you. We could make a deal, if you want permanent access to my library."

"For someone who claims he doesn't make deals with mortals, you seem insistent on making one with me." His words were contradictory, making it impossible to understand what was real and what wasn't.

"You wear the brand of two demons. What's one more?" Jathral tried to sound like he didn't care about my choice, but his eyes burned into mine with desperation.

"I won't make a deal with someone who abandons me, naked and alone."

Jathral's claws scratched the table. "Are you ever going to let that go?"

I crossed my arms. "No."

"You are insufferable."

Jathral seethed, his power pulsing through the air. I was pushing him too far, but I couldn't stop myself. "So are you. Yet, you want me to be tied to you forever?"

Jathral lowered his voice. "You'll make deals with lowly demons like Aburon, not with a demon king?"

My body tensed, fear flashing through my veins. "How do you know that name?" I hadn't spoken that demon's name out loud in centuries. The dream didn't count.

"You told me, little mouse."

My chest tightened as realization poured into me. "That wasn't a dream." That was the only explanation.

"It was an illusion. It was the only way I could check on you with that vampire hovering."

Warmth bloomed in my chest as I thought about the kindness Jathral had shown me. He cared enough to check on me after all. Unless it had been a trick to get his way. My heart squeezed as the possibility poisoned my thoughts. "It was a lie to get me to tell you the name of the demon I had made a deal with."

"No." His voice was sharp. "It wasn't a lie. I didn't force you to tell me Aburon's name. I asked, and you answered."

My hands shook. I hated Aburon, and I hated his name on Jathral's tongue. I never would have told him if I had known it wasn't a dream. "Get out."

His chest heaved up and down. "I can help you."

I couldn't breathe. "If I make a deal with you instead? No, thanks." I wasn't interested in being manipulated by Jathral.

"If you don't break your bargain with Aburon, he will kill you."

I pushed off the table. "If I break the bargain with him, it'll kill me. Without his magic flowing through my veins, I'll die. I'm human, remember? Humans don't live as long as I have."

Jathral turned pale. His anger shifted to something else. He stood, towering over me, but he refused to look at me. "I'm done here. Take me out."

"You don't have to ask twice."

Chapter 23

"Jathral is an asshole." I grinded my teeth together, thinking about the fight with the demon king. Only a few hours had passed, but I felt more heated than during the argument. It felt as if my privacy had been breached.

"Is that news?" Satella inspected her nails as she lounged in the sun. She was wrapped in a large sweater to combat the cold—not that she needed it. Vampires were meant to thrive in the cold, but Satella acted as if the cold was evil.

Aukina stuck to the shade. She wore light clothes made for the summer. She had the opposite issue as Satella. Her blood ran warmer than most land dwellers to combat the frigid sea waters. She thrived in the cold and easily overheated in the summer.

I ignored the tingling in my fingers as my skin begged for warmth. I should've worn more layers, but I had been too riled up to think about that. "He's infuriating, acting like he knows better than everyone."

"You've been talking about Jathral a lot lately," Aukina said. She took a bite of her bread and chewed slowly.

I picked at a piece of food and forced myself to eat it. I wasn't hungry, but I knew if I didn't eat, it'd only make me sick. "He's been a thorn in my side for weeks. I wish he'd conclude his business and leave me alone."

Satella and Aukina shared a look.

"You've been talking about him a *lot*." Aukina wiggled her eyebrows, making me groan.

"You sound like Nyri. I would never want to be with him." I bit my lip, hoping they didn't pick up on the subtle lie. Based on Satella's knowing look, she knew more than I had told them. "Where is Nyri anyway?" It was strange for her to miss dinner.

"Some big romantic getaway or something." Satella waved her hand as if it wasn't a big deal. "So tell us what Jathral did this time that got you so riled up."

I clamped down on my tongue. I hadn't thought my complaining through. Satella knew about my magic causing harm, but I hadn't told her the why yet. For them to understand the why, I would have to be honest with them. The lump in my throat made me hesitate. I didn't like talking about that day, but after years of bottling it up, maybe it was time to finally admit the truth. All of it.

"He wanted me to make a deal with him," I said to ease myself into the bulk of my secret.

Satella scoffed. "What makes that jackass think you'd make a deal with him?"

I took a deep breath, knowing this wasn't going to end well. "When I was young, I made a deal with a demon." Satella and Aukina sat up, not expecting that admission. I kept going before I chickened out. "I was in pain after being burned at the stake, and

I was angry at the world. I hated myself. I hated my village. I think the demon sensed the negativity coming from me. He offered me a deal, saying he would give me the power to get revenge on those who wronged me and to create a better life."

I pulled my knees into my chest as best as I could with my rounded belly. I couldn't face my friends as they stared at me, barely breathing.

"I didn't hesitate to accept it. I didn't bother to ask what he wanted in return. He gave me my magic, far more than most human witches can possess. I felt strong and powerful for the first time in my life. Until I used my magic. I realized that each time I released my powers, it stole part of my life. Just enough to feed the demon, but not enough to kill me. It keeps me alive, centuries past my lifespan while simultaneously killing me. That's the real reason my lungs are weak, and my body is constantly breaking."

The air grew heavy with the silence that weighed between us. Aukina covered her mouth with her hand, and Satella's mouth was pressed in a firm line. I held their stares, waiting for their response. That much new information wasn't easy to digest.

"And what does all of this have to do with Jathral?" Aukina asked, her voice unusually quiet.

I took a shaky breath, which did nothing to calm my nerves. "He found out about it, and he wants me to break the deal."

"Shouldn't you if it's killing you?" Aukina twisted her hair around her fingers.

"I have no control over the bargain. You should know better that the demon has all the control. Even if I knew how to get out of it, that would kill me. My body is sustained by the demon's magic. The moment he decides I don't have another use, then that's it. That's why Jathral wants me to make a deal with him. He wants to be the one in control of me." The realization made my throat tighten. There was so much I wanted to do. I didn't have the right to complain, since I had lived long past my lifespan, but my chest tightened, fear mixing with a sense of doom.

"There has to be something else we can do." Aukina's sweet voice was quiet.

I pulled my lips tight, wishing I had a solution not only for her sake but also my own. "There's nothing to do but wait."

Satella stood, her jaw tight as she looked at me. She walked away without a word. A few months ago, I wouldn't have cared about the vampire's feelings, but my chest tightened as she disappeared.

Aukina grabbed my hand and squeezed gently. "She'll be okay. She has a hard time with stuff like this. Everything with Nyri put her on edge."

I hadn't thought about that. "I'm not dying like that." That was part of why I had kept the secret for as long as I did. The other reason was because I had never had anyone to tell the secret to.

"We're all dying," the mermaid said. "Some faster than others. That's why we have to make the most of the time we have left, no matter the circumstances."

Shadows filled my dreams, turning them into nightmares. Dark claws scratched the back of my brain, taunting me. Panic filled my veins, and I couldn't break free of the grasp that was pulling me into the underworld.

I woke up drenched in sweat. I clasped my neck as I struggled to catch my breath. It was a bad dream, yet I couldn't shake the uneasy feeling churning in my stomach. The air buzzed with power that wasn't my own. Binx meowed on the foot of my bed, pawing at me.

Something was wrong. I wrapped myself in my robe, not bothering to put on a brassiere. I felt the freedom of my chest as I hurried out of my room and into the library. I stubbed my toe on a wooden box on the way out and let out a shout of pain. I limped a few times, but I didn't have time to check the damage, not when there was an intruder in *my* library.

Lights flickered to life as I passed the shelves, following the source of the invading magic. The bookshelves parted for me, leading the way to the black door that led to my personal library. My heart dropped as I saw the door wide open. I reached for the key between my breasts, but it was missing. All of my wards did nothing, but hopefully the hallway had swallowed whoever had the audacity to break into my library.

With a flick, I created a purple ball of light, breaking my promise to not use magic. It was minor magic, but there was a slight tug on my chest. It wasn't enough to do serious damage, but if I found the intruder, that would change. The shadows of the hallway twisted away from the light, revealing nothing hidden among them. The next door was wide open, too.

The room was mostly intact, and the most dangerous items sat in their place, the dust undisturbed. There was only one missing book, and a note sat on top of something wrapped in cloth replaced it. I pulled at the cloth, freeing a dagger hidden within. The black blade had a distinct hum to it, and I knew it was made out of tenisium.

Keep this close to you to protect yourself from demons. I won't be able to protect you any longer.

The lingering scent of snow and winter berries combined with the words made my stomach turn leaden.

It felt as if someone had punched me in the gut. I had trusted Jathral, and it was a mistake.

I moved, unsure of where I was going. My magic crawled beneath my skin, demanding to be freed. I screamed, the sound echoing off the walls of the library. I was going to kill him, even if it'd kill me in the process.

Book stacks flew by me in my fit of fury. The library cleared my path, but then a shelf appeared in front of me. "I'm not in the mood. Now is not the time to push me," I growled. I would never hurt the library intentionally, but I was on the verge of losing control.

The shelf shook, knocking a single book to the floor. The gold title decorated with large swoops caught my attention. I instantly recognized the elven language—one of the many languages I had learned in my lifetime.

A Personal Account of the Northern Elves and the Great War.

"Really? You pick now to give me my book?" I debated chucking the book back onto the shelf, but a breeze stopped me. It ruffled my hair before ripping the cover open. Pages flipped on their own until they stopped near the end.

My throat went dry as I stared at the words on the page.

No.

The book was wrong.

I looked up, unsure where to look when addressing the library. "Why are you showing me this?" The breeze kicked up again, flipping to the final page. I slammed the book shut, my hands shaking.

"Viridian!" My voice croaked as I summoned the master of the house.

Seconds passed before shadows swirled into a figure. Viridian stepped out of the darkness. There wasn't a hair out of place, despite it being the middle of the night. "Do you know what time it is, Miss Tareen?"

"I'm invoking the favor granted by our bargain." My voice was steady, despite every part of my body shaking.

Viridian cocked a single eyebrow. "Are you sure?"

"Yes. Now, listen closely."

Chapter 24

P age 157: *The History of the Northern Elves and the Great War.*

The spell isn't ready, but we're desperate. We've already lost three troops to the darkness. If we lose anymore, there won't be enough of us to defend the weak.

The matron says whoever wields the spell will die, even someone like me, who is considered the second most powerful mage in the clan. Despite knowing that, it is what I must do. It will buy my people time for the demons to figure out a plan to save the world. A noble sacrifice, one I would make to protect my Velena.

I will die, but she will live. She will grow strong and become the next matron. She will lead our people to the future. We had once imagined a future together. If all goes well tonight, that future will be forfeit.

It's okay.

I love her, and I am willing to die for a chance at a better future.

If there was another way—

No. I can't let myself think like that.

If this goes as planned, this will be my last entry, my last words.

Velena, if you are reading this, do not let my death haunt you. You brought me back to life. You gave me happiness, hope, love. For this, I am grateful. For this, I am willing to give you everything in return. Goodbye, my love. I will see you on the other side.

Icy wind blasted my face as Viridian stepped out of his shadows with me in tow. For as far as I could see, the ground was covered in a thick layer of snow. Dark gray clouds hung low to the ground, threatening to spill more white fluff and making it nearly impossible to move.

"I don't see him. Are you sure you brought me to the right place?" There were no signs of the demon king, not a single footprint or mound of snow out of place. I inhaled deeply, the cold air stinging my lungs. The smell of snow was everywhere. If Jathral was there, I didn't trust myself to pick up his scent, especially not with my dulled senses.

"Are you questioning me?" Viridian lifted his eyebrows, looking at me as if I was a fool.

"There's nothing here." The cold wind bit my nose. Hours were all it would take for my body to freeze in a place like this.

"Your eyes must not work." Viridian took long strides, old snow crunching beneath his black boots.

I had to take three times the steps as him. I squinted my eyes in a struggle to see what Viridian implied was nearby, but white mixed with white. It all looked the same. "Instead of insulting me, you could tell me why you brought me to the middle of a snowy plane with no one else here. This was not part of the plan."

"I know what the plan is, Miss Tareen. Maybe if you stop acting like you know better than everyone else and be patient, you'll see that I know exactly what I'm doing." Viridian's tone was even, but his words cut through my soul.

I clamped my lips shut and focused on walking. I should've trusted Viridian, especially knowing our bargain was at play, but the walls around my heart made it difficult to let go, especially knowing what Jathral was about to do, about to sacrifice.

It wasn't long before a cave appeared in front of us. The incline of the hill had blocked the opening to the mountain until we were nearly upon it. It would have been impossible for my mortal eyes to see the cave any sooner, but I decided to keep my mouth shut. I wasn't sure how much of Viridian's tongue lashings I could handle when my nerves were on fire with anticipation.

Viridian stopped a few steps inside the cave. "Are you sure this is what you want to use your bargain on? This is your last chance to walk away and let him face the consequences."

I stretched my fingers open, looking at the marking of a bat etched into my skin. It was stupid to use a favor from a demon as powerful as Viridian on a demon like Jathral. He was an annoying asshole. He left me alone in his castle. He broke his promise and stole from me. He deserved to burn in the underworld for an eternity after what he had done to me.

"I'm sure." I met the Shadow Slinger's eyes, so he knew there was no hesitation from me. There were a hundred different reasons I should have turned around, but the thought of leaving made my heart ache. I hated Jathral, but I couldn't walk away from him.

Viridian dipped his chin in a small nod. He didn't question me again as we moved deeper into the cave. It was chillier than outside, despite the lack of wind. The walls were covered in blue moss that glowed in the dark, allowing us to see as we followed the path to where no outside light could reach. My thighs ached at the incline.

"Why didn't you transport us here?" I asked. My legs were tired all the time from the training with Iolas, which didn't make sense. Training was supposed to make me stronger.

"My shadows don't get along well with the shadows here. If I tried to use them to travel into the cave, there was no guarantee that we wouldn't have stepped out of the darkness and into the walls. I didn't think you'd want to risk that." Viridian's steps echoed around us.

"You were right."

"I always am."

I glared at the demon, but he was ahead of me and couldn't see my disdain. I stretched my fingers, feeling the burn of his magic on my palm. The temptation to make Viridian bow to me with his own magic was strong, but it was a fleeting thought. It was a waste to use the bargain on something like that.

As the moments slipped by, Viridian's footsteps ticking like a clock, my heart hammered against my chest. We needed to hurry. Time was running out, but Viridian didn't look phased. Very little made the demon come undone, and a threat to a king and a kingdom he did not serve didn't make him blink twice.

"Can we hurry?" I whispered, but it didn't stop my voice from echoing in the void.

"It is your legs I am waiting on."

"I'm not in the mood for your insults today, Viridian. I barely slept." I pressed the tips of my fingers against my thumb as I tried to focus on something other than my rising ire.

Viridian took longer strides, making it increasingly difficult to keep up. "I am simply stating facts. If you do not like it, you should've asked someone else for help."

There was no one else I could have asked. Zathrian was the next best thing, but he and I didn't have that kind of relationship. Not to mention, he and Nyri were away on some sort of retreat. This wasn't the kind of thing that could wait, not if my suspicions about what Jathral was doing were correct.

A roaring wind filled my ears, but it didn't touch my skin. The temperature dropped drastically, and every labored breath I took clouded my face. The air grew thick with power that was ancient and wild, even more ancient than the demon kings or the Shadow Slinger. My joints ached from the cold. I liked the cold, but this was beyond what I enjoyed.

The tunnel opened up into a wide room, and the taste of winter berries coated my tongue with each breath. My heart hammered as I scanned the chasm that split the room in half. Wild winds slashed above the cracked floor, coming and going from an invisible force. It would have been impossible to cross it by mortal means.

My feet stopped when I saw familiar black horns on the other side of the chasm. Jathral knelt in front of the stolen book, and his eyes glowed unnaturally bright. His lips moved in a consistent pattern, but his words were lost to the howling wind. Flames erupted from him before getting swept away by the shadows.

The spell was draining his power.

I couldn't breathe. If I didn't find a way to stop him, it'd be too late. I ran to the edge of the crack.

"Jathral!" I screamed until my throat ached, but my voice was lost to the void.

Viridian stepped next to me. "How do you wish me to proceed?"

"We have to get to him."

Jathral was an idiot. His skin grew pale as he continued casting the spell in the book—the one that would take everything from him.

"That's not possible, Miss Tareen. With winds that speed, you'll get ripped from the air if you try to jump." Viridian didn't blink as he stared at the demon king. If he was concerned about Jathral, he didn't show it.

I grabbed Viridian's arm, digging my nails into his sleeve. "I invoke the power of the bargain we made. Use your magic to send me across the chasm, and then you will help finish the spell, so Jathral doesn't have to give up everything."

Viridian's jaw tightened, and his eyes flashed black as the power of our bargain flooded his veins. He had no choice but to follow through with my command. If he broke his side of it, it could kill him.

"Tareen." My name was a low warning on his lips. He had made it clear that using his magic in this cave wouldn't work the same. If he transported me, I could end up in the chasm or worse.

"Do it." My words snapped his spine straight. Viridian gritted his teeth as he fought the bargain. Regret rained in his eyes. If he had known this was how I'd call upon my deal, he never would have made it with me. He underestimated me, which was his fault. I was tired of everyone thinking I was a pathetic and broken witch. "Now."

Viridian's shadows burst from his body. They wrapped around me, stealing the light and the air. The darkness was different without the demon's hand to steady me as I traveled. It was only me in the darkness, and it'd be easy to get lost. I could wander there forever, and everyone would forget about the witch who made deals with demons that got her killed. That path was more tempting than I would have ever admitted out loud. I didn't want to die, but I was tired of everything feeling so difficult.

Heat blasted my cheeks, a familiar heat. It rolled over my skin, as if it was caressing my soul, and I wanted that feeling to last more than the feeling of being forgotten. I followed it out of the darkness. The shadows disappeared, and the soft blue light of the moss lit the path away from me. I was on the right side of the chasm with Jathral only a few feet away.

"Jathral!" I shouted, my voice fighting against the cold air.

His body tensed with the call of his name. He heard me, but it didn't stop him from hunching over the book. His wings were outstretched, blocking his face from me from this angle, but I saw every twitch of his muscles.

"Hey! Asshole!" I moved, desperate to be close to him. If he finished that spell, it would drain him of everything he had left. If what he said was true about not making deals with mortals, then he didn't have as much power as I once thought. Maybe if he was at full power, the elven spell wouldn't take everything, but I wasn't willing to test that theory.

I stormed towards the demon king when he continued ignoring me. Grabbing his arm, I shouted, "Don't you fucking ignore me." Shouting was the lowest level of possible communication with the roaring torrent in front of us.

"Not now, little mouse," Jathral growled between gritted teeth. "I can't stop without breaking the spell."

"That's the point, jackass. Don't you know what that spell will do to you?" The words of the ancient elves scribbled onto the open page gripped my heart. I was confident it was the spell I read about in *A Personal Account of the Northern Elves and the Great War.*

Jathral murmured under his breath, continuing to read from the ancient text. Flames flew from him. Fear gripped my throat as memories of being tied to a stake plagued me. I pushed past them and reached for the demon king again. His skin burned like molten rock, making me yelp.

Jathral ripped his eyes away from the book to look at me and the burn mark I cradled. "Leave. You shouldn't be here."

"Neither should you. If you finish that spell, it will kill you, Jathral. The elves created that spell as a last resort from the darkness. It is powerful, but it will steal the life from you." I wanted to reach for him again, but the stinging on my palm stopped me.

"I don't care. I swore to protect my kingdom. If reading this spell and giving my life means Mithcourt will be safe, then I will pay the price to close the veil." Jathral slid his eyes to mine, swirling with darkness, but it wasn't the kind I had thought lived in his heart. He held the pain of failure close to him, and it dragged him deeper and deeper. He lived alone with no one to save him from his guilt of failure. "Go home, little mouse. Don't use your magic, so you can live a long life with your library. Your bargain won't kill you as long as you keep the magic use to a minimum. I've made sure of that."

There were so many questions swarming my head, but those could come later, after I saved Jathral's life. "No."

"Tareen!"

"Jathral." I dropped to my knees on the other side of the book. I grabbed his hands, grinding my teeth through the pain of his burning hot flesh. "I'm not going to let you sacrifice yourself like some hero."

His chest heaved, his essence flowing from him. It was as if the spell continued working, even if he hadn't finished reading the words on the page. "Why?"

I grabbed his jaw, forcing him to look at me. "Because you broke your fucking promise, and I'm not going to let you get out of it this easily. I refuse to let you die when you haven't begged for my forgiveness. Do you understand?"

"It's not that simple, little mouse. If I don't do this, then my people will continue to suffer." There was a longing in his eyes that broke my heart.

"I don't fucking care. You're not dying. Not until you finish what you started with me. I won't take no for an answer." My heart thundered against my chest. I was laying it all out there, and it terrified me.

"I can't stop the spell now that I've started it." His eyes glistened, but I was sure I was imagining it.

"Good thing I brought help." I glanced behind me where Viridian stood in perfect posture, waiting for my command. "Now." It was impossible for the Shadow Slinger to hear me, but the bargain pulled on the strings between us.

Viridian lifted his hand, and his shadows shot through the air, cutting through the torrent of wind in an impossible way. The darkness parted around me before it came together and slammed into Jathral's chest. He cried out, his face twisting in anguish. Flames burst from him, shifting from orange to blue to green. I grabbed his hands, ignoring the searing pain. The heat warmed my bones, erasing any evidence of the icy world around us.

I sent my own magic into Jathral, giving him more than what the spell required.

"Stop," Jathral barely managed to say. "Using your magic will hurt you."

I ignored the order, even as my lungs squeezed in my chest. "Finish the spell."

Jathral looked ready to argue, but another blast of shadows hit his chest. He heaved as he breathed through the pain.

If he wasn't going to finish the spell, then I would. I craned my neck and began reciting the ancient elven language from where he had left off. Jathral's eyes widened, and he quickly joined me, trying to speak over me. We finished the spell together, and when the last word was spoken, a shock went through my spine as something ripped inside my core.

I screamed from the pain, and squeezed my eyes shut. Jathral shouted, his own pain attacking his body, but he never let go of my hands. The heat from his fire faded, and the tunnel of wind calmed to a small breeze. Icy air licked the sweat that covered me, making me shake. The cold seeped into my body, going deeper than it ever had before. Darkness crept at the edge of my vision. I had pushed myself too hard, but I fought against the shadows creeping in on me.

"Jathral," I whispered, my lungs aching.

"I'm here, little mouse." He pulled me into him, and the scent of winter berries and snow flooded my system, and for the first time in a long time, I felt safe. "I'm here, and I'm not going anywhere."

Chapter 25

"You are taking decades off my life, I swear." Satella pinched the bridge of her nose as she took in Jathral, Viridian, and me. Viridian looked completely fine, except a little more ghost-like than usual.

"I'm fine," I said.

"You're not," Jathral and Satella said at the same time. She held her middle finger to the demon king before moving to grab supplies.

I looked down at my hands. The skin was marred with burns, and even Satella's salves couldn't erase the scars from the blisters. There was no longer a bat etched onto my skin, confirming the deal between Viridian and me had been concluded.

"This isn't a permanent fix," Viridian said. Satella's ears perked, but she pretended to be busy mixing up something. "The veil will begin to tear again."

"This spell will last for a while at least, right?" I said. It had been centuries since the last time the veil split open, threatening the destruction of the mortal realm.

"No," Viridian said, making my stomach twist.

"What about the spell you used before?" I asked. If Jathral's account of the Great Demon War was accurate, then Viridian had sealed the veil once before.

"That was not a spell, and it's not something we can replicate." His tone told me that this wasn't the first time that suggestion had been brought up, and Viridian left no room for additional questions.

"It's not just Mithcourt that's struggling," Jathral said, reading Viridian's face. "It's getting harder for Zathrian to keep Kinzlea safe, too."

I glanced at the master of the house and then at Satella. Neither of them reacted to this information.

"Then what do we do?" My heart hammered against my chest. I had read enough about the Great Demon War to know what dangers lurked ahead if the same fate was repeated.

"There is nothing you can do," Viridian said.

I clenched my hands, but I was instantly reminded of the burns. I hissed, and Jathral's body tensed. "I'm not weak. I can help."

"It's not a matter of being weak," Jathral said. His eyes slid to my hands before finding my gaze. His face held heavy thoughts unknown to me. Questions hung between us and the broken trust and actions of the past day. That was not a conversation to have in front of others, especially not Satella and Viridian.

"If your help is required, then King Zathrian will summon you. Everything is stable," Viridian said, but I heard the unspoken *for now* beneath his concise words. "Until then, enjoy your life as much as possible." The master of the house disappeared in a mess of shadows. He was done with the conversation and had no interest in discussing things further.

"Let me see your hands." Satella swooped in, stopping any awkward silence between Jathral and me. She smeared a salve on my hand, and the burns instantly soothed.

"What's that?" I asked.

"It's the healing salve you made from the bleeding heart lilies." Satella winked before wrapping my hands. "It should prevent most of the scarring, but it won't stop all of it."

"Will there be any permanent damage other than cosmetic?" Jathral asked.

Satella's face hardened as she glared at the demon king. "There shouldn't be. I thought I told you to stay away from Tareen, but here you are, bringing her back to me injured for a third time."

I placed my hand on Satella's arm, but I couldn't move my fingers to grab her. "It's not his fault."

Satella looked at my hand and hesitated. "Why are you defending him? You know what kind of demon he is." She didn't bother to hide her distaste, despite Jathral standing next to her. He didn't argue with her, which was unusual for him. He had been quieter and less combative.

Jathral watched me, as if he was bracing for the insults. They should've come, but my tongue felt dull. He had been willing to sacrifice himself for his kingdom. Despite everything he had done wrong, everything he had done was to save others. Was the willingness to sacrifice enough to call him good-hearted, or was it simply enough to not call him evil?

"I know exactly what kind of demon he is," I said. I licked my lips, knowing that I could never truly hate him.

My answer didn't satisfy Satella. "You should get some rest. We can't afford to have you fall victim to another breathing attack."

"I'll walk her to her room," Jathral offered without wasting a second.

Satella opened her mouth to protest, but I jumped to my feet and interjected. "It's okay."

The vampire huffed through her nose and turned to Jathral. "Don't you fucking hurt her."

"When are you going to learn to trust me, blood sucker?" Jathral flashed his teeth at Satella, but she wasn't phased.

"Never."

"Let's go," I said before the two of them got into it. Jathral curled his fingers into fists, but he didn't argue. He rushed ahead of me to get the door, and then he followed me out.

We walked in silence through the halls of Ethlow. I stole several glances at him, wishing the demon king would speak first. It was our first moment alone since the cave, and everything felt different. The anger and hatred for him was gone. Without them, it left an emptiness in my chest that was filled with longing.

I wanted to hate him again.

Hate was easy.

It was familiar.

Whatever was swirling in my chest was new and terrifying.

We reached the library with a single word spoken. Jathral opened the door for me, letting me enter first. His behavior was strangely kind for the demon, which unnerved me. He lingered on the threshold, even as I walked in.

"This time it was my fault." His words were soft but even.

There was too much space between us, but I didn't move. "What was?"

He motioned to my hands. "Your injuries. You were burned by my fire."

I swallowed hard. I hated the feeling of flames against my skin, but what happened wouldn't haunt me like the last time I had been burned. "I'm the one who touched you. If it's anyone's fault, it's mine."

Jathral shook his head. "Why aren't you yelling at me? I thought you'd call me every terrible name in every language you know for breaking my promise and stealing your book. You came after me and got hurt, so unleash that vicious tongue of yours. I deserve it."

My breath hitched. I hadn't seen this side of Jathral before, and I didn't know what to make of it. I should've been ready to insult him, but I didn't have it in me. Not today. "What did you mean when you said you made sure my bargain won't kill me?" The question had been raging in my throat since he spoke the words, but it hadn't been important enough to ask before.

"I hunted down Aburon and forced him to make a deal with me. He can't kill you through his bargain if he wants to continue to live. It won't stop the magic from feeding on you, so you have to be careful wielding it." He said it as if it had been as simple as going to the market for an errand. "It doesn't free you from the deal, but you won't have as many breathing attacks. There is only one way to stop that entirely, but you have made it clear that you have no interest in being tied to me. This way you can live and use your magic with reason."

My chest tightened. "Why would you do that?"

Jathral stepped forward, letting the door shut behind him. "Do I need to spell it out for you, little mouse?" He didn't stop until he was inches away from me. His warmth brushed my skin, making me feel safe, even as his eyes burned with an intensity that was new.

"Yes," I admitted. I could come up with a million theories, but none of them would matter if I didn't hear them from his mouth.

Jathral grabbed my chin. His touch was gentle but firm at the same time. "Because the thought of you dying makes me want to kill every mortal in sight. If I could ensure you lived forever, I would burn this world down. I would sacrifice my life a thousand times if it meant you kept breathing."

"I thought you hated me." My eyes stung as his words sank in. "I'm just a broken witch."

"You are so much more than that. If you saw you the way I do, then you would see that. If you let me into that guarded heart of yours, I would spend every day proving to you that you are a queen." His scent swarmed me, and his eyes burned into my soul. It wouldn't take much to close the distance between us and let him in, but I couldn't do it.

"Apologize to me," I said. If he dropped his pride long enough to admit his errors, there was a chance I could forgive him and let him in, but he had broken my trust. I didn't care what my heart was saying.

"I don't apologize to anyone." Jathral's words broke something in me.

I stepped back, breaking free from his grasp. My chest tightened, but I wouldn't cry, not in front of him. "Then I'm done." The words hurt worse than his. I didn't want to be done. For whatever stupid reason, my heart wanted the asshole demon king standing in front of me, but my head won. I would not be one of those women who let men walk all over them. Feelings be damned.

Jathral wasn't breathing as he stared at me. I hesitated, hoping the threat of me leaving was enough for him to change his mind, but when I was met with silence, I knew I couldn't stay. I walked away, heading straight for my room. His presence lingered, filling the air with a tantalizing pull on my heart.

I paused before slipping between the bookshelves. I glanced at him and said, "For the record, if that pride of yours wasn't too big for your own good, I would rather be tied to you for the rest of my life than Aburon."

A month ago, I would have told myself I was insane for thinking something like that, but even with the broken trust, I knew Jathral would never intentionally harm me. Aburon would.

Silence met my words, and I walked away, tears streaming down my face. Jathral had made his decision, and I would stand by mine. It was the end of whatever was between us.

Chapter 26

Nyri and I walked through the greenhouse together. She prattled on about her trip with Zathrian, going on about how nice it was to get away and not have to worry about Viridian interrupting them or insisting Zathrian had to get back to his responsibilities as king. The details of the trip blurred together. I could barely get myself to focus on the conversation long enough to remember the specifics. Nyri didn't seem to mind.

There was a heaviness in my chest that had made it difficult to do anything with purpose. It had been days since I walked away from Jathral, but I hoped it would get better with time.

Nyri stopped walking. She stroked one of the petals of the bleeding heart lilies, and the flower perked up, but a frown carved out the young witch's mouth.

"Is something wrong?" I looked at where her eyes were focused, but I didn't see anything out of the ordinary.

"I was going to ask you the same thing." Her hand dropped from the flower. "You seem down."

"I'm fine." It had become my automatic response. Fine was the only choice I had. Jathral meant nothing to me, and letting him affect me now that everything was over was ridiculous.

"You like him, don't you?" Nyri's eyes were bright with understanding. She didn't say a name, but she didn't have to. There was only one male I had spent any time with recently.

"He's an asshole." My heart stuttered. I didn't want to talk about him.

"No kidding," Nyri scoffed, shaking her head. "I'm not exactly his biggest fan, but..." Her voice trailed off as she looked at the ground.

"But what?" I found myself clinging to her next words. I didn't want to talk about *him*, but Nyri was the one who brought him up, and I didn't want to stop.

Nyri continued walking, checking on flowers as she went on. There were new flowers ready to test our next theory any day now, but we were at a loss for how to provoke the purple variant.

"Zathrian said Jathral has been insufferable because of his mood, and he's been in Zathrian's office and room nonstop. It makes it hard to get privacy with Zath. I think he misses you."

My heart punched my ribs, knocking the air out of my lungs. "I don't care." I curled my fingers into my palms, pressing the nails Elcy painted this morning into my skin. The skin was extra sensitive, still healing from the burns, but I didn't care.

"I think you care more than you're willing to admit. I know it's scary to let someone in after relying on yourself for so long but—"

"But nothing," I interrupted. "I was willing to open myself up to him, but he's the asshole who can't fucking apologize. I'm not going to lower myself just because I lo—"

Heat blasted my back, and a familiar power pulsed in the air. "Because you what?" Jathral's voice was a soft caress against my skin, one I had missed.

Nyri took a step back, her eyes widening at the sight of the demon king of Mithcourt.

"Are you spying on me now?" I gritted my teeth as I thought about what I was about to say. If he had heard that, I would have been mortified.

"No, I merely have incredible timing. Now, what were you about to say?" His lips pulled into that infuriating smirk.

"Nothing, because I have nothing to say to you. I told you, I'm done." I turned to walk away, but Jathral grabbed my wrist. I opened my mouth to yell at him, but he was on his knees a second later.

"I'm not done," Jathral said, his voice lowering.

My entire body was frozen, remembering the other times he had been on his knees for me. "I have nothing to say to you."

"Good. Then you'll let me talk. I know I'm an asshole, and most can't stand to be around me, but I fucked up with you. You irritate me to no end, and you are the most stubborn witch I have encountered in my entire life."

"What are you—"

"Don't interrupt me," he growled. "How am I supposed to say sorry if you won't keep your mouth shut long enough for me to properly apologize?"

I lifted my brows. "Insulting me isn't part of a proper apology."

"I'm sorry, Tareen," he growled, his eyes glowing with ire. "I don't regret stealing your book, but I regret breaking your trust. I'm sorry for hurting you. I'm sorry I lied. I'm sorry."

"You're sorry," I repeated, not believing the words spilling from his mouth. Jathral, the demon king of Mithcourt, didn't apologize to anyone, but here he was on his knees for me.

"Yes, now will you fucking accept my apology?" His jaw was tight. It wasn't the best apology I had heard, but he was apologizing. The one thing I had wanted from him.

I bit my lip, my heart and brain fighting. It was too late. He should have apologized days ago when I had given him the chance.

I closed the distance between us and grabbed his horns, angling his head up. "I'm not going to let you off the hook that easily. You're going to have to do a lot of work to make up for stealing from me."

Jathral tensed, but when I cracked a smile, I was met with a smirk. His hands slid up the back of my thighs, teasing right below my aching core. "I think I can manage that."

"Good," I said, my heart fluttering.

"There's something I forgot I had to do," Nyri muttered, stumbling backwards, but we barely heard her.

Jathral was on his feet a second later, his mouth on mine. He tasted sweeter than I remembered. Wind ruffled my hair and tickled my skin. It was as if the kiss had been made out of magic.

I pulled back, realizing there shouldn't have been any wind in the greenhouse. "Wait," I breathed, my heart racing wildly. I looked for the source of the wind. "Nyri!" I screamed.

Her fleeting footsteps stopped. "Goddesses." She ran back towards us, stopping in front of the rows of flowers turning purple. It was a ripple effect, spreading to over a dozen flowers.

"What happened?" Jathral asked.

Nyri looked between Jathral and me, her eyes wide. "True love."

Jathral and I scoffed at the same time.

"You're mistaken," Jathral said.

Nyri smiled brighter. "I don't think I am."

I pursed my lips, refusing to believe it. "It was just a coincidence."

"Uh-huh." Nyri bit her bottom lip, failing to hide her smile. She was going to be insufferable about this. She was too gooey when it came to love and relationships, but it wasn't like that between Jathral and me.

Jathral pressed his hand on my lower back, sending tingles running through my body. "Let's go before she starts spouting nonsense about fairy tales."

"Gladly," I muttered, letting Jathral guide me away from the green house. I risked a glance at Nyri, but it was a mistake. Her smile filled her face, and I knew that wasn't the end of that conversation.

The two of us walked through the forest in silence. A breeze tugged at the few leaves clinging to the trees, pulling them off. By the end of the day, the trees would be barren in preparation for winter. The chill in the air already belonged to the winter months, but Jathral's warmth fought against the elements. He kept his hand on my lower back, keeping me close to his side.

I refused to be the first to speak. In my heart, I knew I had already forgiven him, but I wasn't going to make it easy on him.

Jathral stopped where there should have been no prying eyes, but I caught a glimpse of a crow that wasn't a crow.

"Did you mean it?" Jathral turned to face me, but his hand held my waist tightly, as if he was afraid I'd slip away.

"Mean what? You can't jump into conversations without context." It was hard to hold onto my frustration around Jathral. With his apology, there wasn't much for me to hold against him without pulling at straws.

"You would rather be tied to me than Aburon?" Jathral lifted his brows.

It was a loaded question, one I wanted to run away from. I met his gaze, holding my chin high. "Yes." It was the answer of a foolish girl who let her feelings get wrapped up in a demon that was no good for her. That was something a century-old witch did—not someone my age.

His lips pulled into a crooked smile, and he leaned forward, his scent swarming me. "Then I want to offer you a bargain."

I pushed back the need to instantly agree. "What kind of bargain?"

"I will give you magic and sustain your lifeforce."

"And in exchange, what am I to give you?" I prepared myself for the list of things Jathral would ask me for. My body. My servitude. My library.

"Nothing." Jathral's face softened, showing this was no joke.

"Nothing? That's not very demon-like of you." If it were me in his place, I would've asked for loyalty at the minimum.

Jathral cupped my cheek. "I'm yours, Tareen. To use how you please, but only if you please. I don't want someone who has to do as I say. It'd be no fun if you didn't bite back."

It was hard to breathe as I leaned into Jathral's touch. I wanted his taste on my lips, but I wanted so much more. "Yes," I breathed.

Tension fled from Jathral's body, and he pulled me into a kiss, his tongue begging for entrance. I didn't give it to him. Not yet.

I pulled back, more questions burning. "Aburon won't release me with ease."

Jathral picked up one of my curls and let out a deep chuckle. "You forget I'm a demon king. I always get my way."

Chapter
27

Jathral ran his fingers over the wall, tracing the shape of a door with his magic. Fire melted into the stone walls, but it didn't burn. When he was done, a dark red door appeared in the confines of his magic. He opened it, revealing a portal to his library. "Now you can visit whenever you want."

I kicked my feet from where I sat on top of my desk as I watched him work. "Does Zathrian know about this?"

Jathral clicked his tongue. "Who cares?"

"Does Viridian know?"

Jathral tensed but then he waved his hand. "That old cranky bastard won't do anything to me."

"I hope he does. That's something I'd like to see." I licked my lips as the nefarious thought crossed my eyes.

Jathral huffed, shaking his head. "You are a sadist."

I stopped kicking my feet and shrugged my shoulders. "Maybe a little. At least when it comes to you."

The demon king was unable to hide his surprise. He shut the door before stalking over. He placed his hands on the table on either side of me and leaned in close. "Come live with me in Mithcourt. Then we don't have to deal with other demon kings and shadow slingers. I can take you wherever and whenever I want."

"I'm not going to live with you in that desolate castle." My heart hammered on my chest. Despite the mark on my back—a snake twisted into the shape of an infinity symbol set on fire—I wasn't ready to abandon everything for the demon king, not when I finally had friends at Ethlow.

"I thought you liked being alone." Jathral flashed his teeth, sending a thrill straight to my core.

"Fuck you."

The demon nipped my lip. "Gladly."

He grabbed my hips and spun me around before I knew what was happening. My stomach pressed against my desk as my feet hit the ground. Jathral pulled my bottoms off, and warm air from the demon's magic pressed between my legs. He ran a claw along the back of my shirt, tearing it in two. I'd scold him for that later, but I couldn't find it in me as he spread my legs, opening me up to him.

The demon king dropped to his knees and grabbed my ass. He kneaded the soft skin, making my body ache for more of his touch.

"I like this view of you," Jathral said lowly.

"Don't talk—"

Jathral's tongue slid through my slit, making a moan escape my mouth. He dove in, flicking my clit, and all thoughts left my head. His tongue split in two, one finding my entrance while the other continued working my sensitive bud. The demon knew my body better than any male I had been with, but he had become more efficient, knowing what buttons to press and when.

The pressure quickly built in my core, and I was ready for my release, but Jathral pulled away. An involuntary whimper escaped my mouth, but the demon already had his cock out and was stroking my entrance. "Are you really going to stay at Ethlow when you can have this everyday?"

"Just fuck me already," I begged.

Jathral leaned forward, pressing kisses along the mark that belonged to him. "Answer my question, and then I'll think about it."

I tried to flip over, but Jathral grabbed my hips. He pushed in slightly, but it wasn't enough. I needed him in me, fucking me into oblivion.

"What does it matter where I live when you're here all the time anyway?"

Jathral plunged into me, stopping when all of him was inside of me. "Because you're mine." He held still, making me squirm. I needed more, but he wasn't going to give it to me easily.

"Jathral," I growled.

He nipped my ear. "Yes?"

I grabbed a fistful of his hair and pulled him into a kiss. I slipped my tongue into his mouth, and he came undone. "You're mine, not the other way around."

Jathral breathed me in. "Whatever you say, little mouse."

I kissed him again. "Now fuck me, asshole."

Jathral growled, but he didn't argue. He pulled out of me and flipped me around. He hooked my legs over his shoulders before slamming back into me. He didn't hold back as he fucked me. He grabbed my hands and pinned them above my head as he moved faster and deeper than I thought possible. Shelves shook from the ferocity of our fucking, and when books hit the ground, I didn't think anything of it.

I only cared about the demon buried deep inside of me, fucking me like I had always wanted. Jathral was what I had always wanted, even if I hadn't known it. He was an arrogant asshole who didn't get on his knees for anyone... Except me. I was the exception, and that feeling undid me.

Waves of pleasure crashed through me in a powerful torrent, but Jathral didn't stop. He kept going until he made every part of me come undone. He fucked me against the wall. I rode him on the floor. We fucked each other in bed. It was as if nothing else mattered but the two of us, and for the first time, I understood why everyone was obsessed with love. Having someone that belonged only to me made everything easier in ways I hadn't thought possible.

Even if Jathral was an asshole, he was mine, now and for an eternity.

Author's Note

Thank you so much for taking time to read my book! If you've made it this far, I would greatly appreciate it if you took the time to leave a review on Amazon/Goodreads. As an indie author, reviews are essential for gaining more visibility. All reviews are appreciated! If you ever have any questions, concerns, or general comments, please feel free to reach out to me directly at evereri.theauthor@gmail.com!

ALSO BY EVERERI

Read more in The Demons of Kinzlea

The Demon King's Pet
The Demon King's Cook
The Demon King's Healer
The Demon King's Librarian
The Demon King's Teacher
The Demon King's Assassin

Coming Soon!

The Demon Queen's Rise
Coming in early 2025

The Unfortunate Fate of Mates

Available on the Dreame App:

The Four Beta Brothers
The Stolen Wolf Princess
The Long Lost Luna
The Unwanted Wolf
The Blood Moon Twins

ACKNOWLEDGEMENTS

I am so honored to have all of my friends and family supporting this book series. This has been a series I have wanted to write for a while now, and even though it has been a scary adventure, I have fallen in love with my main characters. They are all unique little beans that challenge me in my writing skills. I have big dreams for this world and this series. I am grateful for anyone who has taken the time to read my book and make these characters a part of your life too.

A special thanks to Mana who inspired Tareen. I know life feels difficult sometimes, but never stop trying.

ABOUT THE AUTHOR

 EverEri is a lover of romance, fantasy, and fairytales, and one of her favorite things to do is to bring a story and characters alive through the written word. EverEri began her true writing journey in the paranormal romance world in 2021, and she never plans to turn back. Whether it's demons, dragons, werewolves, merfolk, or other magical beings, she plans to bring her passions to life in each book she writes.

Want to see more?

Follow EverEri on social media:

IG: everlastingeri

Tik Tok: author_evereri

FB: EverEri's Reading Group

Newsletter: evereri.theauthor@gmail.com

www.ingramcontent.com/pod-product-compliance
Lightning Source LLC
Chambersburg PA
CBHW030319180626
46810CB00003B/1155